BECOMING PINK

SURAIYA MATANDARA-CLARKE

MELLOW PUBLISHERS

PREFACE

In the beginning, when the Founding Father created the earth and the surrounding space, he created three time gods to run the duration of the Earth's lifetime. Their names were Present, Past and Future. They were each given powers, Future was given the power of life, Present was given the power of balance, and Past was given the control over the afterlife. They could not go to Earth itself and were each bound to their dimension. Therefore, together they created a species called the triphants, a nation to live amongst living beings to supervise and act on things the gods would do on Earth. They were controlled by the gods, and had hidden cities called Gateway points. Throughout all this, the gods were given four universal stones that each controlled the extremes of the cycle.

Red was to control realms. Green was to control anti-magic.

PREFACE

Yellow was to control spirits. Pink was to control universal magic. The triphants picked to control these gemstones were called the chosen and their job was the most important of all:

To keep the balance.

Now, the story begins as the balance is disturbed.

PROLOGUE

JAKE

The moment the hooded demon came to the dragon cave, I knew the time had come for me to leave. I had seen it coming from when we had first arrived in Delor, and though I could see the possibilities, I knew I could not change them.

At times, my power seemed to be more of a burden than a gift, but I thanked the gods for it at that moment.

I had seen what would have happened if I had stayed; in that life, we wouldn't have been able to get to Margaret in time. I knew in my heart that Red would save her.

Margaret.

I longed to feel her touch again and see her smile. I felt a pang of regret for being so closed off most of the time.

She had made me forget about the darkness - something so

powerful, that it sometimes consumed my thoughts and tainted my view of things.

All my life I'd felt the demon side of me trying to take over my triphant self; it tugged on my sanity, trying to figure out which side of me was natural. It was a hungry darkness that gnawed at me every day. It was what made me snap at times, and made me so reluctant to loosen up. I was afraid of one day losing control, and in turn, losing her. I would never forgive myself for the one time I did. I hoped that she would be stronger the next time we met, as I knew that would be the only way we could co-exist.

Going with the demon was a risk, but it was a risk I had taken time to think through. It would take me to meet my parents, and that was all I knew. I had done a fair amount of studying at Clorista, pertaining to demons and their ranks. From the looks of it, the creature who was escorting me was a second-rank demon. In their natural state, they were hovering beings covered in dark hoods. They were considered to be deadly and agile, and they portrayed themselves to the human eye however they wanted to be seen. It was mostly mind tricks, but humans had the most malleable thoughts.

I knew that if you were able to take their black heart and crush it, you could kill them.

The portal it opened surged with dark magic and seemed alive in its own way. Though the guilt consumed me when I stepped into it, I felt a hint of excitement. It was my chance to learn about my powers and origins without being questioned. Although, over the years, I had heard many rumours about the demon realm, especially when I was at the Africa gateway. None of it sounded pleasant. As I reached the other side of the portal, my heart skipped a beat. Never had I felt such dread and terror. I was hesitant in taking another step into the realm, but once the golden portal closed behind me, I knew there was no going back.

IN THIS SECTION, magma and red stone were all that existed. The many cries of terror and palpable aura of sadness sent shivers down my spine. Was this really what I wanted to get myself into? I decided not to judge, as I was one of them as well. Though it disturbed me, it was the undeniable truth. I followed the demon as it hovered deeper into the realm and into a dark cave, where it was cold and stagnant. A slight breeze blew through it, giving me goosebumps. I could only wonder where it was taking me, as I had never been here before or even seen it.

"Where are you taking me?" I asked the demon.

"To the queen," it replied in its cryptic language that I could strangely understand.

I gulped, "I want out."

The demon chuckled and said, "Well, young one, you are stuck now and my duty has been fulfilled."

I sighed and clenched my jaw to refrain from saying anything else. I knew the history of the demon queen, how she'd married into the demon society and her husband had disappeared months later. I tried using my power to detect the possibilities, but I couldn't; something was blocking me. I looked around once again at the murky blue sky, red clouds and flying creatures that circled the cave and decided it was best to keep going. I hoped I would survive this encounter with the most deadly demon in the realm and, most importantly, I hoped I would still be me by the time I got out of here.

CHAPTER 1

PINK

I was in the same dark space- trapped once again- a seemingly endless cycle. All I could do was watch as she spoke to them with my mouth. It was wrong- she was using my body as if it were her own and I couldn't do anything about it.

I opened my mouth to scream, but no sound came out. Hot tears streaked down my face as I internally cried for someone- anyone to help me- especially Jake.

I WOKE UP FEELING NUMB, with my sight blurring in and out of focus. I took ragged breaths, the cool air seeping into my lungs.

I currently stared at a glistening, bronze ceiling desperately trying to remember what happened.

Why was I lying here and where was I?

My thought process was excruciatingly slow. Feeling groggy and dazed, I tried to move parts of my body. I needed to feel something- anything. I went from my fingers to my toes.

I managed to steady my breathing and then tried to swallow. When I realised my throat was as dry as sawdust, my breaths quickened again. That's what gave me the motivation to get up, I needed water - or at least something to quench my thirst. To my side were floating lanterns illuminating the grey walls and the dark brown door that was left slightly ajar.

I rolled my legs up and groaned, they felt stiff and fragile. I rolled off whatever platform I was on and fell onto the cold, white marble floor. The cool surface sent shivers down my spine.

"Ah..." I tried to say, but my voice hardly made a sound; it was like it wasn't even there. My throat scratched at me. I groaned and got up slowly, trying to ignore the many creaks and cracks my body was making, like an iron machine that needed oiling.

I COULD BARELY STAND, collapsing as soon as I attempted to walk. With each deep breath, I tried again. After a few attempts, I gave up and resorted to crawling on my stomach. It wasn't a very appealing option, but I didn't have the energy to stay on my feet. As time went on, I felt exceedingly weak and my eyelids grew heavier than ever. With each blink, my eyelids became progressively harder to open, and the burning urge to close them took over.

I eventually stopped crawling and succumbed right back to the consuming darkness.

∽

My eyelids fluttered open and it took me a few seconds to realize I was somewhere else. The ceiling was no longer bronze, but white.

This room was dimly lit but I could clearly see the orange walls.

I looked to my side and gasped as I saw a lady sitting on a red chair reading a book. Even in the scarce light, her skin seemed to glow. She was about a shade lighter than my dusky skin tone. Her posture was rigid and elegant. Her breaths were slow. I watched as her chest rose up and down, admiring the sheer peace she radiated.

She greeted me by saying, "Welcome back, Margaret." She closed her book and looked up to face me.

I looked away. It was rude to stare, but even more embarrassing to be caught. I distracted myself by rising to a sitting position.

Shivers raced down my spine as a draught seemed to pass through the place and my parched throat gnawed at me.

She took up a pale blue cup from the wooden table next to me and handed it to me. "Here, drink this."

Inside was a strange, bronze-colored liquid that shimmered in the light. I eyed it suspiciously.

"It will help get your system working after your slumber," she explained.

I tentatively took it from her and took a sip. It was sickly sweet and had the consistency of milk. After the first taste, I gulped it down in seconds.

"More…" I wheezed. It was all I managed to get out with my raspy voice. I wiped my mouth; she took the cup from me and placed it back on the table.

"What you just drank was enough," she stated.

"Why… am I… so thirsty?" I asked.

All of a sudden, the shivers stopped, and I started to feel a soothing warmth engulf me. I felt the cool energy of my power rush back to me, sending tingles up my spine - I could almost feel the life flooding into me.

Colour returned back to my skin. It was no longer ghostly pale, but seemed to shine; my usual light brown skin gleaming.

"Whoa…" I said as I looked at my skin in awe; not only was my skin colour returning, but a light layer had begun to shed, beneath it was like I had a new layer of skin, glowing and scar-free. Once all the colour in my skin had been restored, I felt my hair. It was getting softer, no longer the coarse texture it had been before. My hair started to curl and obey gravity by lying down on my back; almost like my hair was wet. I could feel the cracks in my chapped lips disappearing and the weight of my eyelids becoming lighter. My sight sharpened and my breaths became steadier.

I felt alive again.

"What was that?" I asked.

"Crystal water," she replied, "It has rich properties that can heal wounds. Since it's so powerful, it can revitalise a person on the brink of death. Hence, it is extremely valuable. I get it from the stream."

An image flashed in my head. A golden river under the clear, crystal bridge from when I first arrived. The fog in my brain had started to lift and I could think more clearly. "OK. That makes sense. So… you're Crystiana?" I asked.

"Indeed I am."

I groaned, stretched from my sitting position and started to get up from the hovering platform. "Oh I wouldn't recommend getting up just yet, you need to give your body time to get stronger."

I sighed and returned to my sitting position. "I still don't get why a nap makes someone so weak and thirsty when they wake up."

She said nothing, instead, her expression darkened.

"What?" I didn't like the expression she had on her face. "Crystiana… how long was I asleep?"

"Well…"

"Well?" My heart had begun to race. Suddenly, I had no desire to hear the answer.

"The darkness in you was still too strong and your spirit was in too weak a state to fight it. If I hadn't done it, it would have consumed you."

"What exactly did you do?"

"I put you to sleep, and it lasted four months."

I gasped. "Four months…" I whispered to myself. "I was

asleep for four months." My eyes widened as I started to process the news; four months of my life had passed by just like that. "What happened while I was asleep? What did I miss? Is Jake back?"

I tried to get up once again but she set a force against me so I couldn't. "Calm down, dear. You…"

I interjected, "Calm down? You practically took away four months of my life - four months I could have spent training or at least getting stronger."

"Listen Margaret. If I hadn't done it, you… probably wouldn't be here right now."

I turned silent.

"I know it's hard to process… being away from reality for so long, but just know I wouldn't have done it if it wasn't necessary."

"I know," I whispered, "Thank you."

I sat there trying to take in the information; she clutched my hands with hers. They were warm and calmed me. She kept them there for a short while as she looked into my eyes. It was almost as if she was studying me. The silver in her irises seem to swirl with curiosity.

"You should get some rest," she said. "Training will start soon."

Despite being reluctant to lie down after four months, I decided to take her advice. I snuggled back onto the warmth coming from the platform and drifted back to sleep.

CHAPTER 2

RED

The murky depths of the inter-realm barrier felt warm and dense. Everywhere I looked there was a dark blue and black mist. It was the only way to the fae realm.

The fae realm.

It was the origin of enchantments. The place I had always longed to visit, from the first time I had explored the capabilities of my gift of enchantment.

At the end of the dark path, a bright beam of light illuminated the entrance to the fae realm. I jumped through and arrived at a meadow full of deep, verdant green grass and an abundant supply of faerie flowers. They saturated the air with their sweet, mellow scents. Minimised faeries fluttered past me and into faerie nests in towering trees. They were robust, circular structures made up of the enchanted bark faeries lived in when they were in their minimised form.

The fiery orange sun shone down on me. It was a refreshing change from the recycled air I had been used to.

Before this, I was subject to the repetitive lifestyle I lived in my chambers. Day after day, I would go through the list of tasks I needed to complete inside of there. Monitoring planet activities in major solar systems, ensuring the space balance was regulated, the gravity levels were stabilized and that the greenhouse kept its neutral conditions. The greenhouse contained plant species I had taken from a plethora of places from across galaxies that I studied for future technology.

Faint whispers were coming from behind me and I turned around to fact the enchanted forest - exactly where I was heading. There were six courts in total, each named after their founding fathers: Bellbon, Tolken, Augustine, Runningbird, Autumn and Ellyon. I had made sure to memorise the fae realm map and nearly all of its known dangers, as well as the useful ingredients I could use for spells and antidotes in the future. I grinned and headed north to Autumn, where I would hopefully find a path to the witch I was looking for, Madella. The witches and the faeries lived together, as they shared similar relationships with Mother Nature.

As I walked further from the forest, the whispers of the trees attempting to lure me in grew quieter. I had heard rumours of the dangers of the forests in the fae realm. Some patches of forest were considered the most dangerous parts of the fae realm, ones that not even the most powerful Fae could stand. So, I heeded these warnings and made sure to stay in the open for the rest of my journey.

Surprisingly, the trek through the faerie field of flowers was quite smooth apart from the tedious batting away of faerie plants and miniature creatures with my telekinesis. However, then I ran into a more pressing issue.

Forest, expanded along the stretch for miles, and, for some reason, I hadn't been able to sense it with my magic until now. I desperately scanned the horizon, along with the map in my head, for a path other than the one which would force me to go into the unpredictable forest, but there was none. I sighed and set my gravity boots to hover mode.

If I was to go into this forest, I would prefer not to be prey to the ground, or whatever it was that lurked beneath the many hues of leaves. From what I estimated, it would be a five-minute walk or a two-minute sprint through the woods. I preferred to draw as little attention to myself as I could. As I hovered quietly over the scuttling creatures and past the snoozing trees, I started to feel growing fatigue, I yawned and my pace slowed. I started to feel as if only a lifelong sleep would be enough to give me energy; suddenly the heaps of multicoloured leaves looked very appealing, almost like a soft bed...

Maybe I should lie down.
Only for a few seconds, to see what it's like.

But, you're so tired...

I was tired, the walk had taken it out of me. My eyelids grew heavier by the second and I sensed my direction change from heading out of the forest to trekking deeper inside, towards a pile of soft, glittery leaves.

Sleep... Sleep... Sleep...

I needed sleep.

I craved it.

I was a few steps away from the pile when I sensed an aura and it disturbed whatever daze I had been in. "Oh no," I murmured.

Where was I?

I looked around and saw I had strayed a long way from the path I had been taking. Who knew how long it would take to get out of this, an hour? A day?

I pinched myself; I needed to feel something. I needed to return my senses to normal. Something had invaded my thoughts, something powerful: something close to me. I edged back once I realised there was a pale pink, glittery haze covering the forest grounds, spreading for miles. I froze as I sensed a large presence from right behind me.

I turned around and saw a towering giant. It had been camouflaging itself to look like a huge pile of clustering leaves.

Giants... greedy bastards that fed on anything with meat. They were creatures cursed with an insatiable hunger. Their abilities included camouflage, supernatural strength, and an immaculate sense of smell and hearing. Their one weakness was being blind. But there was one thing that wasn't adding up. How had I been compelled to come here?

The mind control must have come from something else-something that didn't want me here and wanted me to trigger the giant.

I gasped, the haze, it was the haze - it had led me right to it. I suspected nature in the fae realm was far from normal; the creatures and plants I had come across so far only proved my theory right.

Unfortunately, I happened to come across one of the more painstakingly time-consuming ones, giants. Their appearances weren't easy on the eye, with their dusty rose-coloured tongues, pale purple skin, flat, crooked noses and eyes that looked like they were about to fall out of their sockets. It helped to intimidate their prey. But I had been trained to fight, I had been trained to overcome disturbing, cursed creatures like this.

CHAPTER 3

PINK

I woke up staring at the same bronze ceiling, except this time, my throat no longer burned. I stretched, yawned, and massaged the stiffness out of my neck before sitting up. I scanned the room. Crystiana had left, but something on the beside table caught my eye.

It was a folded piece of paper.

I picked it up and felt it. It was smooth like velvet with intricate patterns. I opened it and read the swirls of cursive handwriting.

'Meet me in the dining chambers.
   ~ Crystiana.'

I frowned. I hardly knew my way around this place, and yet she wanted me to meet her somewhere I had never been.

It was only when I sauntered out of the room, my feet padding on the cool surface, that I noticed the light blue pajamas I was wearing. I wasn't sure when I had changed into this outfit, but it was loose and comfortable, so I didn't bother to concern myself with it. I looked down the corridor outside the room both ways; there was only one way to go since the other was a dead end, just another copper-coloured crystal wall. I made my way along the corridor, brightly lit by luminous gemstones stuck to the walls until I took the only turn available and saw Crystiana sitting in a grand room that seemed to stretch for miles.

The dining chambers.

I looked in awe at the sparkling chandelier with beaming golden lights. It made the room feel ethereal, as did the shiny, golden brown walls gleaming in the light. I discreetly approached the dark brown oak table and sat at a seat farthest away from Crystiana, as that was the only one that had been set, with a shiny white plate and glistening gold cutlery.

She wore a pale blue gown that was decorated with miniature gems. Her silver hair was caught up into a tight bun which accentuated her tight, glowing caramel skin.

As I sat down, she acknowledged me by saying, "Welcome, Margaret. How are you feeling?"

"Finally, like myself," I quipped, "Thank you." I flashed her a smile of gratitude.

"No problem, dear. What would you like to eat?"

"Uh…" It occurred to me that I hadn't eaten anything for a

while. All I felt was an empty pit in my stomach. "I... I don't know."

"Hm... how about some soup?"

"Sure," I said.

Seconds later, a bowl of steaming hot soup appeared in front of me- jolting me out of whatever daze I was in.

The scent of the golden brown liquid drifted into my nostrils, allowing me to get my first smell of food after my four-month slumber. That one sniff was all it took. The empty feeling was gone. Instead, a ravaging hunger took hold of me, and I took one gulp, and the next until I had finished. I looked down into the bowl and the remains of the soup. I was still hungry, but at least I had an appetite now, and I knew just what I wanted to have. The bowl disappeared, and I looked towards Crystiana, who was still sipping at her soup. "Can I get some... meat?" I grinned.

It took four courses to satiate my hunger. "I forgot how good food tasted," I said to Crystiana as I finished a slice of lasagna.

She was eating some steak and sipped on her wine. I took up a white cloth and dabbed any remaining food from the sides of my mouth.

"I'm glad you're back to yourself again," she said, "Now... I think it's time for you to know what you've missed out on. It's not much, but it's best you know."

I listened intently as she told me about Red's venture to the fae realm to save Jake and save the Athen nation- one of the smartest species in the galaxy, how she was still in the fae realm, the fact that Reina was Jake's mother and that there was still no sign of him.

"However, I've been collecting information from some associates I have, around the galaxy. I've only had one lead, but... not to do with Jake and his mother."

I sighed with despair. I couldn't help but feel a wave of disappointment come over me, but I still had to know. "What's that?" I asked.

"There's been a sighting of supernatural activity from a country in Asia. I think it may be the next chosen triphant for Green."

I gasped. I had only met Red, so this was exciting news to me as I could meet another one of my own kind. "I am not sure yet of his current location, but I know he's out there. He's lost and scared. I need to train you so that you're able to retrieve him."

"Of course." I said. "How old is he?"

"I'm not sure of that yet, either. But I will find out. It's only a matter of time before his power shows up again, and that's when I'll be able to locate him. Now, your training starts tomorrow. You need time to adjust to your current state. "

I nodded. She snapped her fingers and the plates and cutlery disappeared, leaving only the two of us at the table. "You may explore the grounds before slumber hours."

"Yes Crystiana." She got up and I could hear the clicking sounds of her heels on the polished wooden floor fade away as she walked. I got up as well, as I didn't like the way the room's size seemed to increase once she had left. In that moment, the fact that I was alone was more apparent to me than ever.

I tried not to tear up about the fact that Jake was missing, or that I didn't know if he was alive or not, by exploring Clorista.

I started off walking down a corridor that was definitely not the same as it had been when I came in. This time, there were a lot more corridors and rooms to go into. It surprised me that she was giving me so much freedom to roam. It was a pleasant change from the restrictions of the orphanage. Then again, that felt like a lifetime ago. And being back in control of my body was one of the best feelings ever. The doors to the rooms were brown and smooth, and they responded to my touch. After a few tries at getting into rooms, I realised I could only enter some, and not others. So far, I had ventured inside one which was dark but with luminous gemstones inside. They were all of different colours, lighting up the room, and a stream that glowed dark blue.

I left that room and walked down some more corridors until I found myself back where I had first arrived in Clorista, the crystal bridge. It was also the last place I had seen Red, another member of the chosen. I kept walking along the clear crystal bridge, trying to ignore the fact that there was a river beneath me. It was at this point that I saw an alleyway leading somewhere beneath it. I walked along the crystal bridge until I reached the end.

I made my way down the steps of the alleyway until my feet were crunching on the different gemstones, but these were different - they were dim and had no inner glow.

When I picked some up, I realised why. The glowing

gemstones I had been seeing had had an energy as if they were alive, but these seemed dead.

Maybe their lifespan was over. This must be where they were thrown out.

Any human looking at these would think they were worth millions, but in this world, they meant nothing. They were mere pieces of rock. I dropped the ones I was holding and went to sit on a ledge which was near the golden crystal water. Sitting down on the ledge and listening to the calming sounds of the river made me think about all the things that had happened.

Crystiana had little to update me on, but the statement, *"No sign of Jake and his mother"* made my heart ache, so the tears I had been holding back finally started to fall. Once they started, it felt like they would never stop, no matter how much I wiped them away. The thought of never getting to say goodbye haunted me. I wanted to think I would see him again, that he was okay, but I just couldn't reassure myself.

I never got to go with him to find Red, and back then, I was just getting to know him. Then, just as soon as he appeared in my life, he left- just like that. Sobs racked my body, and no matter how much I tried to keep my composure, I couldn't calm the whirlwind of emotions. I had lost too many people: my parents, my aunt Rosie, my best friend, maybe even Jake, and I couldn't stand losing another.

But if I had learned anything from my time with him, it was that I needed to be strong enough to save the people I love. I would lose no one else. Finally, the tears stopped and the ache in my heart eased just a little as the realization hit me.

I needed to train harder than ever if I was to stand a chance in this world.

I wasn't sure how much time had passed, but the gentle rush of river had my eyelids growing heavier than ever. I yawned and headed back to my chambers. However, it took me a few seconds to realise that I had no chambers. The place where I had been sleeping was just healing quarters, and I didn't have the faintest clue about how to get back there.

Where was she?

Just as I thought this, she appeared in front of me, in a flowing white gown that had a train and fluffy material rimming its edges. It almost seemed to be glowing. Her silky mane of grey curls stretched down to her elbows, a contrasting hairstyle from the tight bun she had worn before. Her royal blue eyes seemed to pierce my soul and her caramel skin glowing fiercer than ever. She looked beautiful and radiated nothing but elegance and power.

"Hi, Margaret." She flashed me a bright smile full of warmth.

I gasped and stuttered, "Oh sorry, where are my manners? You just look really… really nice. Hi Crystiana."

"Thank you, dear. I hope you've enjoyed yourself. But I'm afraid it's time for bed; you will now see your sleeping chambers." She clicked her fingers, and we were teleported to a room which took my breath away.

Again.

The chambers were designed just how I'd always wanted my home to look. The glistening marble tiles on the floor were a comfortable, cool temperature under my bare feet. I don't know how, but it felt as if I'd lived here forever. The diamond-patterned ceiling was surrounded by quartz walls. Peach opal lights hung from the cream-coloured ceiling, and tourmaline wall lights were set beside the dark oak doors of the chamber. It was a pleasant reminder that in this world, I was royalty. I smiled at the thought of it.

"What do you think?" she asked.

"I think it's the best bedroom I've ever had. I don't know how to thank you enough."

"Don't worry, dear. All you need to do is do your best in training. That would be enough."

"Yes, Crystiana. I intend to." And I meant it - I meant every word.

CHAPTER 4

RED

*I*t made no sense trying to run, as he could smell me from a mile away, but what I could do was confuse him.

I knew one thing for sure about giants, and it was that they relied on their sense of smell more than anything. If I took advantage of that, beating him would be easy. I just needed to steer clear of his hands. I also remembered that one thing on my list was a giant's toenails, so my eyes brightened when I realised that this was my opportunity to get them or at least one. It was a list I'd made in case I'd ever visited the fae realm.

List for Fae Realm:
- *Taolin*
- *Maepi*
- *Tau*

- *Belldrops*
- *Honey Maple Seeds*
- *Bellbon tears*
- *A giant's toenail*
- *Fae moss*

It was barely a few seconds before the impact of his roar sent me flying, clearing the haze. His breath smelled like rotten eggs and fermenting meat. I pinched my nose to stop myself from puking. He launched at me, but I moved before his hand slammed down into the spot where I had been a few seconds earlier. I gasped as he launched again at me, and sent boulders flying towards him, making him scream in pain. I took off my black leather jacket and threw it onto the ground, activating a duplicating spell. Copied versions of my jacket were now sprawled all across a half-mile radius. In other words, he could smell me everywhere and now had lost his sense of direction. The only thing he could rely on was his hearing. As long as I had the hover mode on, I could avoid any trampling of the leaves. The silence was my friend in this battle, and had to be until I made my move.

Soft growls emerged from his chest and I could almost feel his rage as he shifted his weirdly-shaped ears, checking for any sounds. He thought I was his prey, but little did he know that I was his predator, and he had fallen right into my trap. The giants were big and heavy which meant they couldn't move very fast. I now had a plan formulated in my head.

Purposefully, I made noise to make him reach for me, all in the half-mile radius. I just needed to keep it up until the portal was large enough. A trap he would never see coming.

I clicked my shoes out of hover mode; the leaves crunched when I landed on them, and it startled me. As I ran quickly from tree to tree, the giant was able to break through the thick layers of bark with ease. It was as if they weren't even there. I would alternate between bending trees to slow him and being the bait. My speed would have outmatched his, even if he had seen me. By the time the portal was ready, I could hear the giant panting. It sounded as if he hadn't had to chase his prey in a while. I started running in a zigzag direction to keep him confused, then, when I finally reached the location where my portal was, his speed was so fast, that he ran straight into it without a second glance. I held a chipped, pale green toenail invaded with streaks of grey, the size of my hand. The gruesome sight of it sent shivers down my spine, but I mentally crossed it off my list.

- ~~A giant's toenail~~

I sighed, annoyed at the delay, as the portal instantaneously closed. With the snap of my fingers, the duplicates of my jacket disappeared. I didn't need my scent hanging around any longer than it had to. My journey to the Autumn Court would now be longer, but I started trudging forward.

After a few encounters with pixies trying to steal some of my belongings, I finally made it out of the woods. I felt agitated at the delay the haze had caused but coming in contact with the giant had inspired me to use enchantment magic for a protective bubble. It was a new trick I had seen in my grimoire, activated by the word "hai". When I was just about to step onto the plain, I sensed movement from the forest and spun around to make sure there was nothing there. After a few moments of silence, I turned around and continued on the path through the purple grass field. I looked to my left and saw that, a short distance away the ocean was stretching out so far, it blended into the blue skyline. The ocean in the fae realm was tinged with pink, purple and blue hues, each colour more exotic than the next. The wind whipped the curls that were loose from my high ponytail, some red and some black.

As I moved forward the wind seemed to grow stronger and push me in the opposite direction. I knew it wasn't natural and that it was caused by the Autumn kingdom. I climbed up a hill and saw the view of the Autumn kingdom, and the palace in which the Autumn lord resided. I was keeping track of where I was on the map and knew that it wouldn't be too long before I finally arrived.

Crystiana had sent me after a witch called Madella. I knew witches weren't as tricksy as faeries, so it gave me confidence that she would help me with what I needed to know. After all, if Crystiana was sending me to her, she had to be reliable enough to assist. The wind's force only increased as I progressed forward, sending ripples through the long grass. I was coming to a river that seemed to disobey the wishes of the wind by staying completely still. As this was a water source, some faerie creatures were gathered around the sides. There were creatures that resembled frogs but had wings and more intriguing patterns on their skin; they were miniature and passive as their IQ levels weren't as high as faeries.

In the fae realm, the Fae could control their size, from being as small as an ant, to the size of a human. Faeries possessed elemental magic and stuck to the court that suited their ability best. Bellbon and Augustine were the water courts, Autumn and Runningbird were the air courts, while Ellyon and Tolken were the earth courts.

The wind barrier required me to muster the strength I had been reserving from my last portal. I had the spell of a wind bubble so I would not get whipped away by the wind defences; once I was through, I would portal to an area close enough to the kingdom but distant enough that it wouldn't raise suspicion.

The last thing I needed was to get the attention of other troublesome fae who used their powers for no good; the exiled faeries. Ones that had been exiled from their courts for failing to adhere to the rules. They tended to linger on the borders of faerie courts, waiting for any chance to sneak back into the kingdom. I wanted to avoid them at all costs.

MOVING against the strong gusts of wind of the force field was no easy feat. My hair whipped around my face from all directions, making it almost impossible to see. Finally, I made it past the stormy border, with the help of the boots to keep me from being pushed away by the strong gusts of wind. Once I made it inside, I sensed the change instantaneously. The atmosphere was warmer and a lighter gust of wind blew by every now and again. The leaves dropping from the trees varied between brown, red, green, bright yellow, and occasional hints of purple. Trees were scattered everywhere, but not so thickly that you couldn't see the clear sky above. I breathed in the woody scent of musty leaves and fallen acorns. The wind sent chills down my spine, despite my rapid adaptation to the lukewarm temperature. The dry leaves crunched under my boots as I trudged my way across the multicoloured plain. Hardly any faeries lived outside of the border and the ones that did were called exempts. I would try to steer clear of those until I reached the official entrance to the Autumn Court.

CHAPTER 5

PINK

*A*fter she left, I took the time afterwards to soak up the rest of the elaborate details.

On my left, hung a beaming flat television screen on the wall. It gave the time and date and had a gemstone symbol which read, '*100%*'. I went through the mini archway that led me to a gold bathroom. I stood at the curved entrance and looked around while breathing in the sweet scent of vanilla and cinnamon. The wide sink was outlined with gold; on the inside, there were little purple crystals stuck together. The bathtub had brown marble rimming the edges; it was big enough for me to lie comfortably in either direction. Intricate designs were etched onto the porcelain strip that stretched around the bathroom, with hints of embedded gold glistening. There was also a shower behind it, with the light reflecting off its white granite coating and polished wooden handle.

As I left the bathroom, a set of doors facing me caught my eye and I hurried over. As soon as I stepped close, its broad doors opened automatically. My eyes shone with excitement as I realised it was a walk-in closet, with a theme of checkered marble and dark oak wood. Clothes I had never seen before were on the hangers. They looked like training outfits; despite them being black, they each had complex patterns.

I walked further in and saw layers of shoes which all looked convenient for training and running. There were also some normal shirts, skirts, jeans and dresses - most likely for if I ever needed to blend in with the humans on Earth. It seemed so long ago that I had been staring at the dresses in the shops in awe. It all seemed so trivial now, especially when I'd witnessed some of the true evils in this world.

I opened the first drawer of the chest and found cotton pyjamas inside; there were six different designs, and two pairs of each. I took up one that was patterned with swirling vines and blooming flowers with mocha-coloured embroidery.

Satisfied with everything, I started heading out, until I caught a bright glow in the corner of my eye, behind the levels of shoes.

After finding a way to separate the shelves holding the shoes, I saw the source of the flashing light. It was simply the light reflecting on a polished mirror. It was a decent size, much bigger than me. My eyes lingered on my reflection. I hadn't really paid attention to my body in a while, but I had started to develop curves. My face had grown sharper and my stare was cold and rigid. I'd lost a lot of weight and the meal I had just eaten showed clearly in my bloated stomach. I lifted up the side of my shirt slightly and I could see the imprinted lines of my ribs. I took a deep breath and brought the shoes back together, covering the mirror once again, then swiftly headed out of the closet, hearing the doors shut softly behind me with a click.

There were sheer curtains covering large windows and I pulled one to the side to see a bright, glowing orb in the just beyond which illuminated the space around it. It was evident that wherever we were, was in the middle of a galaxy. Many stars surrounded us, with pink and green fog complimenting the darkness of space. My eyelids quickly grew heavy and fixed back the curtains to head to the bathroom to get ready for bed.

After fiddling with the settings of the pipes, I finally figured out how to run a warm bath. I left the mirror behind the sink fogged up with steam from the hot tub and went into the closet to put on the pyjamas I'd chosen,.

Climbing onto the hovering platform, I realized it didn't feel like I was hovering four feet above the ground and I might as well have been on a bed on the ground. Its sturdiness rid my fears of falling off. I pulled the pale pink sheets over me- glad to finally be in my own space.

The little bit of walking had tired me and sleep tugged on my eyelids. Soon, thin borders of silver-tinted glass emerged slowly from the sides of the silver platform. I tested my weight on them and they held their position. I took one look around the room and then snapped my fingers. Nothing happened. I sighed. Maybe I had expected too much from the magical experience. I got up again and when I did, the silver-tinted glass barriers went down immediately. I padded over to a glowing amber button on the wall and pressed it. The room transformed from its golden hue to dark blue, with gentle beams of colourful lights dancing around the room. They bounced back and forth in waves, and I fell asleep watching them.

∼

I woke up feeling refreshed and well-rested. I don't know how, but whatever was lighting the room made it seem like daytime. I didn't know exactly where Clorista was, but I knew that whatever was outside of the halls and the magical rooms was a never-ending space. The silver-tinted glass shrunk down as I got out of bed. I stumbled into the bathroom and yawned, looking into the sparkling mirror. I looked at my face close up and saw that it had a faint glow. Once I had finished in the bathroom, I went to the walk-in closet; the clothes I had seen on the rack yesterday were gone, and only one of the training outfits remained. It was a leather jumpsuit decorated with pink embroidery.

The jumpsuit hugged my skin, and the snug material kept me warm. I strapped on a pair of black boots and headed out of my chambers. When I looked down the corridor, I saw it led straight to a room. I wasn't sure which one.

I wondered if we would eat like humans, three meals a day. I felt as if the one meal I had had the day before could last me days. When I reached the entrance of the room, I realised it wasn't the dining chambers. It was a room with bright fluorescent lights embedded in the ceilings. There were polished wooden floorboards and the walls were padded with light grey material. They felt firm and bouncy, the perfect material.

Could this be where I would be training?

There was a black circle in the middle of the polished floor. It seemed to be useless at first, but in a matter of seconds, it sent red lasers across to me, as if it were scanning me. I didn't realise what was happening until it was too late. The lights shut off immediately, and I was left in utter darkness. I started to panic; I could feel the darkness creeping on me. By instinct, I searched for my gemstone. I called for it with my magic and felt a barrier. Crystiana had done something to it.

I felt a strong surge of fury that I had to rely on my own instincts to get me out of this. I knew triphants were able to see in the dark, but as much as I tried, I couldn't see in this darkness; even though I knew it was probably just a setting of the training room, I couldn't help but feel helpless and vulnerable. My inhalations grew sharper. It felt like I was being squished and in a large space at the same time.

When I finally heard Crystiana's voice, it echoed around the room, sounding like she was both in front of me and beside me at the same time.

I kept looking around as she said, "Welcome to your first training session. These first few sessions will be more like tests to help me identify where I need to assist you and your strong points. Today I will be testing your instinct and senses, so your training session will be in the darkness. You will not be able to see, so use your other senses to the best of your ability. Remember that you are safe within these walls, but that does not mean you will not feel pain; pain is an imperative part of your training, as it imprints on your memory and helps you to focus on techniques to survive and stay out of the path of danger. Good luck, Margaret."

I don't know what I had been expecting, but it certainly wasn't that. I had expected reassurance, maybe even an apology for putting me on the spot this way. It was neither, and I felt more frightened than ever; she had just said to use my other senses but hadn't told me what was coming. It was the unknown that scared me, and that was what she was testing me on.

I didn't realize why the lack of notice was bothering me so much, until I thought back to previously, when she had made me feel safe and secure - like nothing could hurt me in Clorista. Now, she had thrown me in the middle of a survival course and said I would feel pain. I had expected to be trained - to learn combat – not to be tested, and that's what made the horrible feeling in my stomach even worse.

My heart was beating frantically, so I focused on my breathing.

In and out.

In and out, and that's when I heard it: a giant thud from somewhere on the right side of me. The sound dynamics had changed. It was as if I was outside. I started to move away from the sound, whatever it was, I knew it wanted to cause me harm and I didn't plan on getting attacked in the first few seconds of the "test".

I heard another thud coming from the same direction and then I turned to move in the opposite direction. Then there came vibrations, I could feel the wind moving through the free strands of hair from my high ponytail. I contemplated leaving the hair down or just putting it into a bun, then decided that would take too long and kept moving. I prayed I wouldn't bump into anything.

I gathered the magic inside me, channeled it into a ball and split it between my two hands. I stretched out my arms and felt the things in front of me, I could feel nature, so I knew now that I was outside, navigating my way through some sort of field. If I had been in a forest, I would have bumped into trees, or maybe even tripped over boulders. I allowed the energy balls to dissipate into thin air.

I kept a steady speed, moving in the same direction until I felt a resistance. I couldn't run any further in that direction, so I turned to the right, away from whatever was chasing me. There was no sound, so I stopped, maybe they were never chasing me.

That's when I felt a change of temperature, the place felt more humid, and I felt a light rain. I sighed, "Great."

I was going to get wet.

I was still engulfed in pitch-black but felt the cool drops of light rain. A wind blew past me, and shivers ran down my back. The light rain rapidly got heavier and heavier until it was bucketing down onto me. I had to think of a way to protect myself from it. I couldn't see anything so the rain blurring my eyesight wasn't a concern, but I wanted to stop the rain from drenching me. I started to feel the water rising, swishing against my boots, which fortunately turned out to be waterproof. The sloshing of water told me that I was either outside, in a place prone to flooding, or I was inside a confined room which meant that there was only a certain amount of time before it filled up and cut off my oxygen supply.

I recalled Jake and I having a conversation about how the triphants' respiratory systems could purify the air around them so it is safe to breathe. I started to wonder if there was a way I could make a shield using my powers. Maybe there was a way I could somehow use the water to form a shield around myself. I closed my eyes for the sake of it, and focused on the thrum of power pumping through my veins under my skin, and letting it flow from me. I used it to feel the presence of water and its memory. I tugged on those particles and lifted them up to build a shield around me, I felt them obey my command; the water swished and built itself up to form a bubble around me. Once I felt the rain stop falling I knew the shield technique was working; I had a bubble formed around me. I kept it up for a few seconds and then released it.

If I hadn't done that, I would never have been sure that I could use my powers like that. I could now form water shields, and maybe shields with other elements. I had a connection with nature that I would forever cherish. I sighed and opened my eyes. I could see pure darkness once again. "Please let that be the last test," I repeated to myself. The ground, or whatever I was standing on, started to shake and I began to feel uneasy. What was going to happen next?

CHAPTER 6

RED

The day was overcast, with lilac clouds hovering over the court. I referred to the map in my head to keep track of how close I was and pulled on the enchanted cloak to hide my magical presence. The last thing I wanted was to capture the attention of all the witches in Autumn Court.

It had always been modelled after the season with piles of leaves that were metres deep. Trees with confused colour palettes and pale blades of grass.

When I reached the top of the hill in the leafy terrain, I was able to see the maze walls that prevented any random person from getting inside. If I hadn't had my portals, it would have been much more of a feat to get to the entrance. In the corner of my eye, I caught a glimpse of a rapid movement.

It had to have been a member of the exiled fae; while I was more powerful than them, I didn't want to stick around long enough for a fight as that would be a waste of the limited time I had.

Once I spotted the blossoming burgundy roses from the swirling ivy that was wrapped around the sparkling, steel gates, I portalled right to it.

I walked through the darkness of the interportal realm once again, and, while there was a slight resistance, when I got to the other end, I was in front of the gates.

They opened automatically and I strolled in, trying not to attract too much attention. But of course, it wasn't every day someone made it past the infamous Autumn court labyrinth with little to no injury. I was an exception and that intrigued them. I sensed them near me but portalled away before they got the chance to speak, leaving the pungent smell of dung behind me. The poorest members resided near the entrance; the wealthier a faerie got, the more they moved up the social ranks, and the better their accommodation. I had portalled to an alleyway in the centre of the court, the busiest part of it. It was also known as the middle-ranked section, and most of the Autumn court fae resided there.

Being in a more crowded place gave me the coverage I needed as an outsider. I joined the flowing crowd in which everyone wore either purple or green.

I still followed the glowing red circle in my head, which indicated where Madella's was supposed to be hiding out. Being one of the most renowned witches meant she had to have little to no imprint in the fae realm. It was the sad reality that the witches lived in, but I suppose it was the survival of the fittest. The strongest witch was the most hunted, primarily because, when a witch killed another, they absorbed their magic and their strength grew.

According to witch history, the more magic you possessed, the more spells you could perform and that worked in their favour. I'd imagined she'd spent years perfecting her protection in case any other witch managed to invade her property.

I kept my head down most of the time, but I studied as much as I could from the limited vision I had. In each court, there was a certain dress code for the creatures that resided in them. For Autumn, only biodegradable clothing was worn, and they were not to be bright colours, but more pale and dull. However, the fae tended to overdress or wear little to nothing at all.

There was an abundant source of moon and sun dust in the fae realm, but the Autumn court had done the most to integrate it into their culture. In the day they wore sun dust, which shimmered and lightened up the space around them to spite the overcast day and elevate one's motivation to be kind and relaxed. By contrast, moon dust was a sparkly substance that acted as the human equivalent of glitter.

While it got everywhere, it stimulated happiness and glowed in the dark. I had read somewhere that the fae loved to spread it on them at night and have parties all night long. It was rumoured that the Autumn court lord, Lord Theo, was the kindest lord of all and I had a feeling that the abundant source of space dust had something to do with it.

The fae had quite extravagant tastes when it came to how they styled their hair. Some of their traditions mimicked those of the triphants' which is why some had their hair done as if it was flowing in water. There were gemstones placed symmetrically along their shiny hair from their roots to the ends. Once the fae reached the peak of their powers, they were able to control their size. So I had to make sure not to trip over some of them, while others towered over me. There were leaves scattered on the patterned, stone ground that ranged across all colours. Just like humans, the faeries owned pets. They were carried around with magical leashes. They were peculiar creatures that could do much more than cats and dogs, like communicate with their owner. However, the one thing they had in common was that the creatures they called pets were also domesticated. They were tamed in such a way that the owner had complete control over what they did from birth.

From what Crystiana had told me, Madella lived in an old trinket shop. As I travelled further north, the place grew more desolate. Soon I had escaped the crowd and I was amongst the higher-ranked fae. They didn't concern themselves with the lower ranks, which was fortunate, as otherwise, it would have been a lot harder to sneak in. You could tell the difference between lower-ranked villages and the higher-ranked ones. It was as if everything was richer. The air was crisper and the smell of the spices was more potent. The scents of nutmeg and cinnamon wafted through the air. The richer fae could afford more and obviously spent more money on their décor. The fae made money off trade and secrets. In the fae realm, secrets were worth a lot; the higher ranked the faerie was, the more they would pay for them. Others made it a darker way, exploiting powerful witches for the sake of rank and wealth.

I scurried across the street to the abandoned alley as I felt the last pair of eyes lift off my cloak. Their attention was focused on the products that the middle-ranked merchants were selling on a floating display.

It was growing dark quickly as it was already dusk. Orbs had materialised and were casting a warm glow over the village. I walked down the alleyway, taking off the hood of my cloak to get a better view of the place. There was no shop. I frowned and double-checked the map in my mind. At this point, I felt a presence behind me. I whipped around but, before I could attack the owner of a gnarly nose and wrinkled, lilac skin, I blacked out.

CHAPTER 7

PINK

No matter how much I squinted my eyes, all I could see was pitch black. The ground was still rumbling so I crouched. It wasn't long before it stopped and the atmosphere grew even more humid. Beads of sweat trickled down my face. The ground beneath me morphed; it felt grainy, almost like sand.

Was I in a desert?

That would explain the drastic temperature change. I attempted to stand, but couldn't; instead, I sank further into the ground. Judging by the grainy texture around me, it didn't take me long to realise I was in quicksand. I paused to think about the best thing to do. I knew that the more I moved the deeper I would go.

I felt like I had been sitting in this puddle of sand for eons, though it could only have been a few minutes. I grew flustered. I couldn't sit here forever, something bad was bound to come my way. The heat was growing more unbearable by the second; while my clothes had dried from the water, they had become clingy once again thanks to my sweat. I felt helpless, so I closed my eyes and meditated. As I searched my mind for answers, I had flashbacks to my last encounter with sand, when I got taken away from Jake. It had been the last time I ever saw him. I shivered and my heart raced. Sand scared me.

I knew that I couldn't afford to freak out: not like this, I was now chest-deep into the sand, with the rest of my body buried underneath. I took a deep breath and released my magic to feel the sand's essence. However, the strangest thing was that I couldn't. I couldn't sense the sand, it was as if it wasn't there, even though I could feel it physically. I took another deep breath and tried again. After several tries, I realised that maybe I just couldn't control the sand.

That's when I heard her voice. It reverberated around the space as if it was coming from everywhere at once; she said, "You cannot control sand because it is not an element. Instead, you must manipulate it."

My eyes widened as it started to make sense. I ran through the elements in my mind: earth, water, fire, ice, light, darkness, air. "Air." I couldn't help but grin at my breakthrough. I could use the wind to lift the sand. I concentrated on the air around me and gathered a gust that came rushing around me. I felt it as it lifted the layers of it. Soon, the sand had been removed from my waist and I was able to wriggle until my body was out of the quicksand and onto more solid ground. After I had tugged my feet out of its grip, I dropped my control of the wind and collapsed onto the ground, panting.

After a few seconds, I could see light streaming through my eyelids, which could only mean that the lights had been turned on. I opened my eyes but quickly closed them, as the light burned my eyes. Instead, I opened my eyes slowly, using my hand as shade. Soon, I could see something other than blinding white; I could make out a figure – Crystiana. Today she was wearing a dark blue gown with a moon-crescent pattern and crystal heels. My voice was scratchy as I spoke to her. "How did I do?"

"I'm impressed." she said, "I classified your powers, they resemble Ameliora's. I can also tell you discovered some things about yourself too."

I cleared my throat and said, "Yeah… I did, and I don't think I would have if you hadn't burdened me with this surprise test." I smiled, but then frowned, "But… I do have a question." It was a topic I had wondered about, but never had the courage to ask.

"Yes, dear?"

"You know how you found Red?"

"Mhm."

"How did you find my mum?"

"Well, she…" She paused for a while and then sighed, "She's my daughter."

I gasped, "But if she's your daughter, then…"

"I'm your grandmother."

"When were you going to tell me this?" I asked, trying to wrap my head around this news.

"I know it's a lot to take in," she said, "I was going to tell you, I just didn't know when, and there was never a right time. But... I suppose now you know."

"I'm your granddaughter…"

"Yes." There were tears brimming in her eyes. "And you have no idea how long I've wanted to tell you. I've waited for this moment for so long - too long," she said.

"I… I don't know what to say," I said; just seeing the tears in her eyes made me want to burst out crying too. "I thought... I thought you were dead." I sniffled.

"I know, dear. It was for the best."

I stood and she took me into an embrace. At first, I was tense, but then I melted into her warmth. Her bony figure was surprisingly comfortable, giving me the reassurance I needed.

Once the warm embrace was over, she smiled through the tears, and said, "Now dear. It's up to you how you want our relationship to continue. If you want me to be just a trainer to you then that's up to you, but if you want us to have a proper relationship as we are, then I will promise to be the best grandmother I can be." Her eyes stared into my soul as if searching for an answer. I wondered what she would find as I wasn't sure of it myself.

"I think I want…" I realised that I had to think about what to say. I knew I wanted a relationship with her, but I also knew how important my training was. I didn't want this to get in the way of how hard she would push me. I continued, "For us to have a relationship, a bond, but instead of going easy on me, I want you to go harder on me than you have on anyone else." Her eyes seemed to light up.

"Margaret, dear. I would already have done that no matter what you said. Just know that sometimes you will hate me because of what I put you through, but it's because I love you dearly and would hate to see you get hurt in this unforgiving world."

"OK…" I paused. *What would I call her?*

She must have sensed my distress and figured out my problem because then she said, "Call me Grammie. I always wanted to be called that if I ever had a grandchild."

"OK… Grammie." I smiled, "I like it too."

"I think you should get some sleep or at least head to your chambers. You did well today, but we'll talk more about it tomorrow."

"OK."

~

I BATHED AND HAD A SHOWER. Then I sat in my bed, contemplating the day. I was too shocked to process it all, but realised that the tears welling up in my eyes weren't happiness or relief; they were the product of confusion and betrayal. My heart ached for the truth.

Was everything a lie?

Was the life I had lived before just a cover-up of who I truly was?

"I need to know. I must find out," I whispered to myself.

After a while of brooding on the topic, my mind drifted to something else.

She had said she would be testing me on multiple things, and that was only the first one. She had said the tests would revolve around my senses: my instincts. I thought back to when I had been restricted in my sight, and could only see black; it seemed so long ago but yet it was so recent. I had been exposed to what it would be like without sight and in a way, it helped strengthen my other senses.

I knew whatever Grammie was doing was for the best and it would help me in the future. After witnessing a bit of what Red was able to do with her powers, and how confident she was, I was determined to become like that and more.

I hummed the soothing lullaby my mum had always sung to me until I felt sleep tugging me.

I was exhausted.

CHAPTER 8

RED

When I regained consciousness, I was in a dimly-lit room on a bed almost as soft as the hard cloud I had slept on back in my chambers. I felt dazed and heavy.

Had I been drugged?

I studied the room and realised the light was coming from pixies. I got up steadily and headed over to get a better look at them. The black, mouldy floorboards creaked despite my cautious steps.

Though the pixies were trapped in lamps, it didn't stop them from threatening me with their fire magic at me. I was surprised to see them in person. Fire pixies were rare and very destructive. It was smart to keep them locked away to serve the purpose of providing light, but was it cruel?

Of course.

Their bodies glowed yellow and they wore sunset orange, leaf dresses. The three of them were females, all with striking, auburn hair. One had her hair in a bun, another had hair that flowed to her waist and the last had a wild mane of curls. I looked away from the mesmerising swirls of their deep orange magic and looked around the room some more. The bed I had woken up in was in the corner of the room; next to it stood a bookshelf with dusty books.

It was safe to say this room was neglected and ancient. I began to get a pressing feeling that I was being held as hostage. I spotted a desk that was also gathering dust, with a pot of blue ink and a white feather. Beside the desk was a door I couldn't seem to portal past. I got a whiff of an aromatic bush and followed the scent to see where it was. There was a good amount of bushes all potted with a mix of different plants. I recognised one of them, Taolin. It was a plant with swirling brown vines that protected its sacred fruit in the middle. The fruit possessed the ability to cause paralysis. Its centre was yellow and its sides were emerald green. It grew directly from the ground on a faerie full moon. A faerie full moon occurred every two months. In the fae realm, the moon was pale red and the sun was fiery orange. This was because, in the ancient days, the founding Red had been the one responsible for creating the fae realm, so the sky had a permanent film of her magic over it.

I snatched the fruit off of the plant and was about to portal it to my chambers, when I sensed the absence of my gemstone. I felt it somewhere around and opened a portal to it but when I tried to take it, an unfamiliar pricking sensation stung my hand

and I pulled it back immediately. I chanted a healing spell on the throbbing red spot that had appeared on my palm and slowly but surely, it disappeared. To say I felt agitated was an understatement, I needed to get the gemstone back as soon as possible. I didn't know how it had been taken, or who by, but I wanted them to pay for it. I could feel my magic rise to the surface as my fury grew. I had never faced these limitations on my power before and I wanted to know how and why this was happening. I heard creaks coming from outside and conjured a ball of magic. It floated readily in my palm.

I could sense the faerie magic coming from the Taolin and the other plant species huddled next to it. Somehow, though someone or something was near, I couldn't sense their aura. It was like there was some sort of spell or device that was blocking my magical senses. The doorknob turned and I grew still, the portal ball swirling silently in my hand. A witch entered the room, carrying an opal tray with a few condiments on it. I noticed her swirling, silver irises first, then her sharp, pointy ears that peaked out from underneath her lengthy, thin golden hair. Her patterned, pale green skin looked smooth in the dim light and her dress was patterned with the intricate drawings of the witch culture.

It was only then that I could sense the considerable amount of magical power she possessed. I kept my composure as this could be Madella. "Who are you?" She frowned and I realised that she couldn't understand me. I immediately switched to speaking in the fae language. "Who are you?"

"I'm Saphella," she responded, her words clipped. I had never heard that name before but it had a nice ring to it. "Answer my questions, Saphella. Why can't I access my gemstone? How are you blocking my triphant senses and where is Madella?"

I watched as she tentatively placed the opal tray on the desk, her gaze never leaving the decent-sized threat I had swirling in my hand. "My mother will be available soon. For now, you should make yourself comfortable," she declared. She turned to exit the room but I threw the sparkling portal ball inches away from her, causing her to jump and the cream wallpaper to sizzle. "Answer my questions."

"My mother knows a lot about the triphant race. She spent a lot of time studying them after Crystiana came. To answer your question about your triphant sense being nullified, there is a spell that she created for that specific purpose." That explained why I hadn't sensed whoever had knocked me out.

"You know Crystiana?"

"Yes. Well, no, not directly."

"Interesting."

She paused and asked, "Not that I need to know, but how do you know her?"

I wasn't sure of the type of person she was yet so I persisted, "You first."

She paused for a bit and started, "When my mother was pregnant, a witch cursed her and it was all she could do to stay alive, much less give birth. But thankfully Crystiana saved us. She broke the curse and nursed her back to health. Now you tell me."

"She's my mentor… or was. Do you know what happened to my gemstone?"

"She put it into an enchanted cage."

I internally groaned, as an enchanted cage was one of the most powerful protections you could come across. Once an enchanted cage was created, the only way to retrieve the thing inside was if it came out by itself or the person stopped casting the spell. That meant that there would be no hope of getting back the gemstone until she let it out. However, I had some peace in knowing it was safe from any other forces of the universe that wanted it. I guessed I would just have to threaten Madella into giving it back to me.

"I should get going now. Also, don't try using your time magic to follow me, there's a barrier behind the door so it would prevent you from leaving anyway."

I considered the possibility that she was bluffing but remembered how I had tried to portal out and failed. So, instead of debating with her, I sighed.

"Make sure she knows I'm waiting and I have an urgent matter to discuss with her. Tell her it's something to do with the demons."

"I'll make sure to." She left and the door shut with a soft click behind her. I sighed as I was once again left with the persistent chatter of the fire pixies.

I sauntered over to the centre of the room, where I could see each of them contained in thick, enchanted jars in their different locations. The one with the bun was placed on a vacant spot on the dusty bookshelf, the one with the free-flowing, wavy hair was on the wall opposite and the last was on the desk.

"What are your names?" I asked them.

"What is it you want of us, triphant?" The one on the bookshelf spat.

"I just want to know who you are and how you got here." I remained passive so there was nothing they could say against me. The fae always looked for trouble and created mischief in whatever way they could.

"Why would we tell you that?" The one with a bun said.

"Because I'm your only hope of getting out of here," I said. I knew that would get their interest.

"We saw your portal magic," said the one on the desk. "You're one of the chosen, aren't you?"

"Yes, I'm Red. Nice to meet you."

They all nodded, then the one with long, wavy hair announced, "My name is Saraphina, but you can call me Sar."

"Clover," said the one with the mane of curls.

"I'm Natasia, but call me Nat."

"Sure. Now, tell me how you guys got here and… what happened to the rest?"

"They perished in a pixie war," Nat said.

"I'm sorry to hear. How did you guys escape?"

"We… never participated."

"Wasn't it mandatory?"

"It was but we'd gone to a witch festival to help the witches kill Madella," Sar said quietly.

"Why would you help the witches?"

"They said they would help us defeat the water clan if we helped them... They didn't live long enough to keep that promise and we were captured."

"It was my idea," Nat murmured, and her facial expression tightened and her light grew dimmer.

"At first, Madella used us as lamps in her study but we made too much of a fuss, so she took us down here. We've been here ever since." Clover said.

"That sounds awful."

"We lost everything and we didn't even get to say goodbye," Sar said, clearly in grief.

"What caused the war in the first place?"

"Our pixer found out something he wasn't supposed to about the water clan," Clover explained. A pixer was the pixie equivalent to a king; one command from their mouths dictated what the pixies did.

"So, I'm guessing the pixer of the water clan started the war?"

"Yes," they said in unison.

I didn't know much about the pixie world but I knew the legend of the fire pixies was over 300 years old, and that they held significant power despite their size. "The fire pixies became extinct 300 years ago," I announced and all three of them gasped.

"I didn't know it had been so long..." Sar mumbled.

"How are we still alive?" Clover asked.

"It's possible Madella put an eternity spell on you."

"So we would be punished by being the only ones left of our kind for the rest of our lives until we're killed..."

"Look..." I paused and the atmosphere grew thick with tension. "A war is coming and I need all the help I can get."

They looked at each other. "He's back, isn't he?" Clover asked; I knew exactly who she was referring to. Though I had my suspicions, I wasn't sure and I wanted to make sure I didn't give them too much to worry about. "We're only sure that Reina is making moves that could destroy the balance."

"I don't know..." Nat said.

"Nat, we've been locked up for so long... Wouldn't it be...?"

"I don't want to come out of this hellhole just to go into another."

"Wait. I still haven't said what it has to do with any of you yet."

"What's that?" Sar asked.

"I believe there is a way for you guys to help without fighting on the battlefield - it's the safest option."

"How?" Nat asked.

"Defense," I suggested, "You would come with me to free another set of allies, who would help us with the attack. No battlefield involved."

"Promise?" Clover asked.

"You know I can't guarantee that."

She sighed.

"I'm sick of being in these jars. I want out." Sar declared.

"I'm with Sar on this one." Clover agreed, "What about you, Nat?"

"I..." Her expression grew grim and I could see she was conflicted.

The last time she had made a decision like this, it had got them trapped in jars for 300 years. "OK."

"Good." I smiled at her, then said, "If anything, use this opportunity as a way to avenge your people. You're not to attack Madella, but fight to make up for the time when you didn't." They all grew silent; the only sound was my heart beating.

I couldn't ignore the emptiness in my stomach any longer; my gaze landed on the tray Saphella had left with a pale red cup filled with steaming, murky green liquid and something that looked like toasted bread. I was ravenous after using up so much magic to open a barrier portal. As I was separated from the continuous source of magic from my gemstone, the magic I'd used to create the portal ball had sapped much of my energy. After drinking the sweet, minty liquid and munching on the delicate crunchiness of the bread, I crawled back into the bed and slept, leaving the fire pixies to discuss whatever they had in mind. If I'd learned anything over the past few centuries, it was that nothing was guaranteed, so I took my chance to replenish my energy while I could.

CHAPTER 9

PINK

When I woke, I felt refreshed and ready for training once again. My room glowed orange as a sign that it was dusk. The light was streaming from the curtains. I drew them open and saw the same glowing, orange orb in the middle of blue space.

Its glow was enthralling, but the more I stared at it, the brighter it seemed to get. After a while, my eyes began to throb, so I closed them again. Even though I knew Clorista was a realm in space, I had to wonder where it really was.

After stretching, I made my way to the bathroom. The mirror showed me the sizzled ends of my hair. I searched for some scissors and found a pair of mini black ones. I started to snip away the dead ends and ended up cutting away two inches of my hair. I had never had hair this length and took some time to take in my new look.

Afterwards, I had a quick shower despite longing to soak in a hot bath and went to get ready for my next training test. I wet and brushed up my hair. I found a sticky substance next to it, which I could only assume was hair gel. There was no time to question it; I knew that the sooner I did this training, the more time I would have to myself – or so I thought. Given Crystiana's training strategy so far, I might never be sure of what was going to happen, and maybe that's how she wanted me to think. I should always be ready for anything which comes my way.

I picked a training outfit made of a matte material outlined with leopard print in glossy spots. I strolled to the doors and rested my hand on their cool surface. Once they sensed my presence, they slid open and I exited the chambers. I was once again on the same strip which led me straight to the training room. A feeling of dread passed over me but I pushed on, knowing it was necessary for me to get rid of my fear of the unknown. "I'm here!" I called out; my voice was absorbed by the sound pads which prevented any echoes. Crystiana, or should I say Grammie, appeared in front of me with a gentle smile. Today she was wearing a white gown lined with fluff around her neck.

"Good morning, Margaret," she said, "How are you feeling, dear?"

"I'm good... Grammie." I smiled and hoped that it wouldn't always be this awkward. "I was wondering... Where is my gemstone?"

"Ah yes. Your gemstone is safe and locked away, if you want to see it, you can after training."

I sighed, "OK then." After staring at me for a few more seconds, as if taking me in for the first time, she started, "Alright, well… Yesterday you were tested on what you would do without your sight, but say one day you lose your hearing from a loud accident or explosion. What would you do?"

I gasped and was about to say something, but she disappeared as quickly as she came. I closed my eyes and took a deep breath, I would have sight but no hearing.

"I can do this," I whispered in an attempt to motivate myself.

When I opened my eyes, my sight was fuzzy but after a short while, it sharpened. I was in a charred field on a planet that didn't look like Earth. It had trees the size of skyscrapers, an orange-tinted sky and red ground. Alien creatures were running around everywhere in a state of panic; beside me was Red, her eyes glowing and her stance fiercer than ever. She was holding some kind of barrier between the creatures and us. My instincts told me something was wrong, that I should turn around. At that point, I saw a huge black rock speeding toward us, I panicked and took slow breaths trying to think of something I could do. "Red! Look!" I shouted.

She gasped in response, threw a huge force towards the alien creatures and attempted to get to me swiftly, only she wasn't fast enough and the rock landed right where Red had just been. The ground vibrated harshly and the force threw me far away from her.

I hit the ground hard on my back, and the breath was knocked out of my lungs. All I could hear was a ringing sound. I knew that this was where my test would start. Although a sense of sadness resonated within me, I knew that if this was real life, she would not have gone down so easily.

However, this was my test and that was why she couldn't stay alive to help me. I got up, slowly but steadily, trying to conserve my energy. I knew she would not go easy on me, but from the last test, I had learned that, though it might be unpleasant, I would learn more things by myself as well.

As I stood up, the scenery changed and the red ground changed into soft, moist dirt which had plants scattered across it; trees filled the barren land, and soon it became a cool forest. The atmosphere had changed from humid and dreary to refreshing and crisp in just a matter of seconds.

I took in the scenery and started to walk around, a slight breeze blew past, lifting some leaves with it. They danced in the air with their fluttery movements. The ringing had stopped and now all I could hear was pure and utter silence. However, my few moments of peace didn't last for long; it was replaced with a sudden feeling of dread. I searched around until I saw huge rocks barreling toward me. I gasped and my heart raced with fright, I knew I had to think fast.

They were gaining speed; in the few moments I had left, I used my magic to raise a thick blanket of hardened dirt as a barrier between me and the hurtling rocks. I closed my eyes and sensed the rocks with my magic. I grabbed hold of them and clenched my fist, imagining them being crushed together. I imagined them to be stronger than ever and channelled all my will into that. I felt the harsh vibrations of the rocks barrelling into the towering wall. I released the breath I had been holding and the grip I had on the earth. It collapsed back to its original form - loose, gathered dirt on the ground. I was quivering from the amount of energy that had taken. I had only needed the wall to protect me from the stones, which it had. I had expected it to break from the impact the rocks would have at the speed they were going at, but the wall had been so strong, it had been able to withstand the impact of the rocks.

I wiped some sweat beads from my forehead and turned around, away from the rocks. I expected to see more forest, but in the time that I had taken to defend myself from the rocks, a black cave had appeared. I walked tentatively onto the rocky cave floor. I noticed the rocky walls of the cave were glossy. I ran my hands along the surface; the rocks were particularly moist.

After taking a few steps into the cave, a sudden wave of humidity hit me, but my suit regulated the temperature. I smirked at the new feature I had just discovered. "Cool," I muttered to myself. I started to walk deeper into the cave. A clear substance was dropping slowly from the top of the cave; as I watched it drop, I tried to imagine the sound it would make if I could hear it. Having no hearing made me imagine a lot of sounds, like in the forest, I had thought about what the trees swishing side to side would sound like. Now I had been thinking about what my feet would sound like on the rocky subterranean ground of the cave.

As I walked deeper into the cave it got darker, but in this darkness, my triphant vision worked. I closed my eyes and felt my magic course through me, the cool rush of familiar energy running through my veins, eagerly waiting to be used. I envisioned it in my palms, bouncing around as a light source, and when I opened my eyes, there it was, my magic floating around in my palm. Soon I realised that the magic ball in my palm wasn't the only light source I had; the leopard print on the sides of my suit now glowed pink. It was like it had been activated when I used my magic. I grinned and continued walking. The dripping of the substance continued, and only my thoughts kept me company.

Even though it was a simulation, it felt strangely real. As I was walking, something on the cave wall caught my eye - it was a symbol. I hovered my magic ball close to it, and it illuminated more of the black wall. Once I had illuminated more of the symbols, I frowned and recognised them; they were triphant language. Although I could speak it, I had yet to understand the symbols. I was sure I would learn how to in my future training sessions. I didn't know how to feel about not knowing my own language of origin, but then again, I had thought of myself as a human until a few months earlier. That made me think: what month was it? Which day was it?

I kept the light on the symbols, trying to understand what they meant. I felt my hand gravitating towards the symbols; soon I was touching them. I closed my eyes and soon regretted it, I saw flashes of horrible things, mostly death. It was caused by something, something in the cave. I gasped when I realised I wasn't alone. Even though I didn't understand the exact meaning of the symbols, I understood what the message portrayed - it was a warning. I glanced at something in the corner of my eye. It was glowing purple.

I held my breath and turned slowly towards it. The pressure of not being able to hear anything was getting to me and I was becoming more paranoid by the second. The least I could do was make sure the movements I made were as subtle as possible. I could only see the creature's refulgent purple eyes; they were piercing my soul.

It was an animal that resembled a tiger, so I could only imagine the vicious growls it was producing. It took a step forward with its enormous paw, the rest of its limb shaking from the force. It looked like it was growling, with drool dripping from the deadly fangs at the side of its mouth. I could tell it was acidic from the way it ate away at the rocks as soon as it landed on them.

From its agile posture, I assumed the creature had experience in hunting. I also sensed a considerable amount of power. Its expression grew even fiercer so I assumed I had somehow made it angry. The only reason for that would be because I was in its domain.

I took a step backwards, but then felt something behind me, a warm breath. My heart stopped. There was another one. Gradually, I managed to inch myself to a spot where I could keep an eye on both of them: two black tigers with glowing purple stripes, and murderous intent plastered on their ragged faces.

It was obvious that whatever I did next would be essential to my survival, and one thing for sure was that I needed to get out of there - away from them. My heart was racing as I figured out the only way I would stand a fighting chance; first, I would have to calm down.

I closed my eyes and took a deep breath. It was easier to ignore the tigers because I couldn't hear them, but I could still sense them, and that was driving my pulse haywire. I gasped and my eyes flung open. I could control elements, maybe I could control the rock somehow. As soon as I came up with the idea, one of the tigers pounced at me and I shrieked with terror. Maybe it was on instinct that I was able to use the rocks of the cave to shield myself from the attack, but whatever it was, I did it just in time and gave it a huge graze on its side. I had made them angry, especially the other one, who was now more determined than ever to get at me.

My moments of shock were over, I now had to focus. As I had predicted, the other one made a move towards me. It lifted its paw, aiming right for my face. I continued to use the swift technique of gliding the rocks to where I wanted them to go. Sometimes I used them as a defence by turning them into a wall for the tiger to hit instead of me, and other times I would use them to attack. After a while, I got used to the movements and they became fluid, soon it was just the rocks and me, with the occasional vibration from the force of the tigers. The vibrations got weaker and weaker until the force suddenly stopped.

I had been so caught up in controlling the rocks and using my power that I had not noticed the brutal injuries the tigers were suffering. One of them barely had the strength to get up and the other was using the little strength it had, to lick the wounds of its friend. Maybe if I could have heard their cries, I would have stopped, but unfortunately, I hadn't been able to. I felt remorse at seeing their fragile state. Before I knew it, tears were forming in my eyes. I moved towards them but the tiger stopped licking its friend and attempted to bite me. That was enough to tell me that they were done with threatening me; they didn't want me anywhere near them. I wiped the tears from my eyes and set off to find my way out. I realised that I didn't need my glowing orb of magic because of my adapted vision; that was clear enough to keep me going. I hurried to get away from the tigers, and the narrow passage of the cave soon became a broad expanse. It felt so empty yet so mystical like there was a deeper meaning to it.

It led me to wonder where the tigers had come from. Even though I was walking out unscathed, I didn't feel triumphant at all. I felt guilty. I had only wanted to avert their threat, but they had been so harsh and aggressive. If I hadn't acted the way I did, maybe there would have been a different outcome and I would be in pain instead. To make myself feel better, I reminded myself that this was only a test – an advanced simulation designed to make things feel real.

I stopped walking and thought about where I was going. I didn't have my hearing so I had to think beyond that.

What could I do with my abilities that would help me find a way out?

It just came to me; I needed to put my hand on the wall, to feel the connection between me and the rocks - the history. As I felt the wall, a familiar energy rushed through me, and it felt like the most natural feeling in the world. At that moment, I realized what I needed to do.

CHAPTER 10

RED

I woke up to a faint humming noise and jumped up. I refused to be caught off guard again. The humming only grew louder until it was right behind the door. I watched as the doorknob turned and as it was pushed gently. It was Saphella, I was both relieved and annoyed as I wanted to get out of this room as quickly as possible. "Follow me," she instructed. I had many things I could have said to retort to her bluntness, but I decided to stay mute and waved goodbye to the pixies. I followed her up the sandstone steps and the door swiftly swung shut behind us.

"I see you've met the fire pixies," she began.

"Yes, they're a nice company," I replied curtly.

"I've known them since I was little."

"Didn't you ever think to let them out?" I asked.

She scoffed, "I can't let myself out of this prison, much less others." The way she described her home as a prison had me wondering how it might look. But, when we reached the top of the steps, I felt insulted that Madella had given me that small room. I took in the ruby red carpet on the floor, the grand pillars that held everlasting fire to keep the light and the gallery along the walls- filled with paintings of powerful past witches. It seemed Madella had used her magic to create a sophisticated underground palace in the centuries she had been hiding. When an alden passed me, fully dressed in a suit, I realised that Saphella wasn't the only magical being here. Aldens possess the characteristics of frogs except for their abnormally big size and their ability to talk and walk. "Hi Walter," she said to him.

"Hi," he murmured; he seemed in a rush at the pace his little legs were going.

"Wow..." I whispered, mesmerised with the way the drawings on the ceiling moved to create different types of art.

Saphella headed towards a door and I watched as the alden waddled away into the distance. We reached an aluminium door; I watched as she turned the doorknob and signalled for me to go ahead. When I walked inside, various scents of plants wafted into my nostrils, some pleasant and some acrid.

I followed Saphella and recognized plants drawn in my grimoire. I spotted maepi, bayn and moss. They were all on my list of things to retrieve from the fae realm. We'd gone past so many different plants, I'd begun to lose track; at one point, I believed it was an underground forest. "How did you get so many plants?"

"My mother sends out our servants to collect them; welcome to her greenhouse."

"She's here?"

She nodded, "This is where she spends most of her time."

The temperature was humid, and light beams streamed in through the thick, shimmering glass like there was sun outside. We turned a corner and I switched my boots to gliding mode as the thick jungle vines stretching across the floor became too tedious to look out for. Saphella had obviously been here many times before; the vines didn't bother her and she would slash them with her magic every once in a while. Hovering lifted the burden of walking.

Why had it taken me so long to use it?

Beyond the many bushes, I could see a slender figure.

Was that Madella?

Excitement rose within me, as I was about to meet a grand witch, a privilege not many had. I especially wanted her to teach me the many things she'd learned in her years of expertise. I heard the figure's voice humming a sweet tune with their melodic voice. I was intrigued by the way she was able to weave magic into her voice and asked, "Is that Madella?"

Saphella nodded in response and I sped up, only slowing when I reached her. Her strength in enchantment clearly beat mine by a long way; I enthusiastically said, "Greetings, Madella. I'm R..."

"I know who you are," she interrupted.

"OK," I continued, "I'm having a dire issue and Crystiana told me you could help me."

Her left eyebrow rose when I mentioned Crystiana; she said, "Go on..."

"I was told you know about Reina. I need to know everything you know about her." Her expression darkened at the mention of Reina.

"Anything else?" she asked.

"Well... two things."

"Speak."

"My gemstone, I'm going to need it back. Also, I would love to know more about enchantments, it's one of my gifts and you're renowned for your expertise in it."

"Ah... Your gemstone. Your abilities resemble those of a witch, I cannot let you have an advantage over me. Just know that it's safe where I have it."

"I know where you have it, but knowing who I am you must know the importance of me protecting the gemstone. If you didn't know already, I could tear this whole place down without it."

"Are you threatening me in my own home?" Her voice went an octave lower and I knew I was treading on dangerous ground.

"I'm simply explaining the extent of my ability."

"Hm..." She flicked her fingers and the enchanted cage appeared hovering in front of me, with my gemstone inside of it, "There you are, but I trust you know what's inside."

"An enchanted cage," I said through gritted teeth.

"And only I can unlock it. You may have your gemstone all

you like, but you may not access its power until we are finished and you are out of my territory. Are we clear?"

"On one condition."

She raised her eyebrow in response.

"If your territory is invaded while I'm here, you unlock it when I say to unlock it."

She paused. "OK." The whole time she had been concentrating on dissecting a fae fish; all I could see was the side of her straight nose, shaped brow, chiselled collar bones, powdery pale green skin and luscious dark hair the shade of a raven.

Her hair stretched to her waist and curled at various points. I knew she had to be at least a century old, but she had aged down to look as if she was in her thirties and the wrinkles seemed to blur into her skin. Her lips were full and plush and her cheeks had a healthy blush to them. It wasn't very obvious but I could tell she was using a glamour spell to cover her ageing. "My daughter mentioned something about a war to me. Is this true?"

"Yes. A major attack happened on Nubur, home to the Athen. The demons were somehow able to break through the barrier and go to another planet, where they stole a valuable jewel. When I went there, I found a survivor and they told me that Reina was responsible for the attack."

"Let's discuss this over tea, shall we?" she suggested. I nodded in agreement.

She made a gesture with her hand and the lab clothes dissipated to reveal a long, flowing red gown that hugged her curves and accentuated her pale green skin. She clicked her fingers and we arrived in a room full of a potent aroma. "You may sit." I sat

BECOMING PINK

on a chartreuse loveseat and observed the pink wisps floating around the room.

She wrote some glowing symbols in the air and I recognised them as the witch language that was strictly for spells. A few seconds after she blew them into the air, a gnome came waddling in. I watched as she swiftly whispered instructions to it and as it exited. She sat and stared at me for a while as I studied the map on the ceiling.

It was a map of her palace. It seemed to expand all across the underground of the Autumn court. It had me wondering how she had been able to hide in such a big place for such a long time. There was a light green, glimmering circle around a place called, *"The Loungerie"* and I assumed that was where we were now. The loveseat seemed to get more comfortable with each second that passed. When she asked, "What's your real name?" I knew what the wisps of scented smoke were.

Their sweet scent was no longer therapeutic, but suffocating as I recognised them as the overpowering scent of truth serum. She had been diffusing it into the air all this time.

This must be where she questioned people.

It made it the perfect place for her to have a discussion. It made me realise the depths of her paranoia, but I didn't blame her. "Melenia Toxiel," I replied reluctantly.

Names granted power in the witch world and that wasn't something I had intended to give out lightly. A smile tugged at her lips when she caught me eyeing the wisps of smoke suspiciously. "It's a nice trick, isn't it?"

I didn't give her the satisfaction of saying "yes". I just rolled my eyes.

"Now dear, you already know my name, it's only fair I know yours." I felt like I was being held hostage and the only thing keeping me sane was knowing that my gemstone was safe.

If she ever betrayed our agreement, she would pay dearly.

"How do you conceal such a large place?" I asked, seeing if the truth serum would work on her.

"If you're trying to make use of the truth serum, don't bother. I've already made myself immune to it a thousand times over. You're the one being interrogated here."

I clenched my jaw to prevent myself from saying something I shouldn't. She continued to ask me questions about my life as a triphant and I gave her short, clipped answers. I may only have been able to speak the truth, but that didn't mean I had to tell her all of it. Her gnome came back holding a clay tray of two steaming cups of the minty green liquid Saphella had given me before. She caught my hesitation and assured me, "I didn't poison it."

"I still don't trust you." I knew I would have said that even without the truth serum in my system.

"I know." She sipped on her tea and continued, "Reina… Reina, Reina, Reina."

I raised an eyebrow and she sighed. "We crossed paths a long time ago, though it seems like yesterday. I will never forget her face because of what she did to me." I watched as her face turned into a scowl. "She was a striking beauty," she continued, "She had come to the fae realm by a Lord's pass."

"How would she be able to...?"

"Hush now," she said, "Once I finish, you may talk."

When I nodded, she continued, "She came to me asking what spell was keeping her son's magic from being sensed. At the time, she seemed like nothing more than a distressed mother, seeking help from a renowned witch, but I should have known better, for she used my pregnancy against me. She manipulated me into helping her because of what we had in common, but she did not know that I could not have cared less about the so-called freedom she had to offer me, for that freedom would have been detrimental to Saphella.

As she was not a witch and was simply passing through, I gave her my name, as I felt bad for not accepting her offer, and it cost me." I watched as her facial expression tightened and her eyes turned cold. "By giving her my name, she was able to pass it on to another witch, who cursed my pregnancy and almost took my own life with it. She thought I would die – and I would have if it hadn't been for Crystiana. She saved Saphella and me. I will forever be in debt to her, but she said I could repay her by doing her a favour in the future, and I suppose you're that favour." She looked me in my eyes with an intensity I wasn't used to, but I held her gaze. "If you say Reina is behind this upcoming war, I shall do everything in my power to stop it."

"It seems you knew Reina as a triphant, while I know her as a demon."

She frowned. "Explain your encounter with her."

"I only witnessed her actions. I did not see her."

"Her actions, then."

"Somehow, she became the demon queen, used low-ranked demons to invade Nubur and capture the athen in the capital city. As I said they also stole a jewel that the athen valued dearly. It's called the Morova."

"I haven't heard of that thing in centuries…"

I shivered internally. "I think she may have been a part of the dark triphants, and I suspect she may have made a deal with *him*." From the sheer disturbance in her expression, I knew she knew who I was referring to.

The Dark Lord was one of the darkest forces ever known to this universe. Some even say he was the origin of darkness, but he hasn't appeared for millenniums.

"For now, we must suspect the worst and do what we can to develop our forces. From what I gathered, Reina is a very ambitious individual, who will not stop until she gets what she wants," she suggested.

"I agree," I pursed my lips and continued, "What faerie lord did you say gave her the pass?"

"I am unsure; she wouldn't say, but whoever did is a betrayer to the fae realm, so we must be wary of all the fae lords."

I nodded.

"You will need all the help you can get against this new evil," she said, "For now, my second-in-hand will take you up to your room so you can get cleaned up."

I watched as an oak door appeared in the pale wall that had ivy growing over it and as her second-in-hand entered. I gasped as I recognised the pale, wrinkly lilac skin. "You're the one who captured me," I said.

He gave me a wry smile.

"Normally I can sense magical beings from a mile away. How were you able to catch me off guard?"

"It was a spell, it dulls your supernatural senses," he explained calmly. His deep voice was scratchy. He watched as I pursed my lips and assured me, "It was the safest way."

Though he was calm and collected, there was something about the glint in his milky eyes that rubbed me up the wrong way. Madella continued drinking her tea as we left and walked in silence to my room. We passed the dank staircase that led to the pixies' room and headed to a different section of the underground palace. This section was outside. We walked on a cobblestone pathway; the luminescence of the sapphire blue lake had a soothing effect. "It's beautiful…" I whispered.

"It's one of Maddy's favourite places in the palace."

"How did you guys meet?"

"We met at a witch festival a couple of centuries ago."

I scoffed. I had no idea why they named it so formally when everyone knew it was a public massacre.

"So you knew her when she got cursed by Reina, right?"

His facial expression tightened as he said, "Right."

"What are you?" I asked as I studied his frail state. With his patchy silver hair, he could pass for an old man on earth if it weren't for his lilac skin. "I'm a warlock."

"Ah…" It all clicked together at that statement. A warlock is often the protector of a witch. They share blood bonds and, unless the witch dies from a natural cause, the warlock will die too. Unlike witches, warlocks are more powerful in groups and can often channel magic from each other. But his situation was different, as I doubted she let him out much. "I don't recall you telling me your name."

"Razel." His words were becoming clipped. I knew the only reason he told me was that witches could not curse warlocks and vice versa. Even though I possessed similar powers to a witch, I did not have a connection with nature and I didn't resemble them in the slightest, so I didn't consider myself one of them. "OK," I replied and ended the conversation there. Despite him wanting the best for Madella, I still didn't trust him and I often trusted my guts. There was something wrong here and I was going to find out, even if it was the last thing I did.

CHAPTER 11

PINK

At first, everything seemed normal until everything around me, including Crystiana, faded away into black fog, and I was left alone.

"Hello," I said, to see if Crystiana was still there, but my voice was swallowed into the black smoke and there was no response. After a few seconds, I could hear the faint whirring sound of a machine as if it was being turned on. After that, there was silence, ringing in my ears louder than ever.

Soon, I saw a dim light growing gradually brighter. I could make out more details after a few seconds and realised it was a bright, fiery red ball coming towards me at full speed. There was no time to run and I barely had enough time to duck. After that, one after another came at me. I kept dodging them one by one, sometimes at the same time. After a while, I got too used to it and let my guard down, so when one was hurtling right toward me I didn't notice it in time so when it was just a few inches away from my face, I instinctively put up a shield for protection. The flame dissipated immediately as it came into contact with my shield, but then I realised that I had used my magic. I had broken the one rule Crystiana had given to me. I sighed, but then I realised that being used to using magic had made what was an easy task even more challenging.

Instead of just a few coming at a time, one after the other, it was a group coming at the same time, one group after another. It was as if she was punishing me for using my magic.

Not only that, but they seemed to be speeding up. I did a good job at dodging the first few groups, but I realised that after dodging for a while, I was starting to get tired. Without my magic, I had seemed to revert back to my unfit self. I didn't have much stamina; it was only sheer determination that kept me going.

Ball after ball, group after group, light after light. I steadied my breathing and concentrated on the task at hand. As the pace got faster, I knew I had to find a way to conserve my energy. Most of the balls were coming at chest level, so I crouched to minimise my contact with them, but that was even worse. In fact, it was the worst thing I could have done. As soon as I crouched to a lower level, the fiery balls came straight my way; now, they were no longer coming above me, they were at my stomach level, and the amount coming toward me had doubled, and that's when it happened.

As I moved downwards a ball sped towards me, and before I

could react, it hit me in my stomach; it was like a brutally intense punch.

That's when I realised that the fiery balls weren't made of fire at all; the light was just disguising the fact that they were a bunch of punches, a bunch of fists. Then I gasped, if this was a real match, then the opponent would change to where I was to attack me further. All the time the fists had kept me from moving, and, because I had been so caught up in dodging the fists, I hadn't seen the source. It was a bright light that wasn't too far away, although it would be difficult to get to.

Once I realised, my strategy changed. I started to move forward as well as defend myself as I counterattacked the fists. After dodging, getting punched and parrying punches for what seemed like ages, I saw that I was getting closer to the bright light. Seeing the distance between me and the bright light diminishing gave me the hope that I was going to make it, and soon.

I had a burst of adrenaline coursing through my veins; for a while, I saw a pattern of all the things I needed to get past the obstacles. As time went on I was able to get the hang of the routine, and soon it was almost like a second nature. It was still a shock when I finally reached the bright light.

At this point, the fists stopped and all was quiet. I felt the soreness in my body easing, as I was drawn in by the mesmerising beauty of it. It was not just a light, but a ball. A ball made up of pulsing, warm energy. My hand drifted toward it, but, as soon as my palm felt its warmth, the darkness around me started to fade and I was back in the brightly-lit training chambers. It took a few seconds for me to adjust to the environment, but soon I made out a figure which I knew was Crystiana.

"So... how was it?"

"Well... I definitely learned how to dodge, and I'm a lot quicker at it than I was before."

"That's great - exactly what I wanted to hear. Did you figure out what the balls of fire were?"

"Yes... I did. They were fists, weren't they?"

"Yes, they were," she admitted. "OK, now for the next one."

I gasped, and the aching and soreness of my body returned, "But..."

"Hm?" Crystiana asked.

"Nothing." I sighed, and mumbled, "Here I go again."

The orange dots reappeared across the chambers and once again Crystiana tapped on the Combat one with the same image of two people in a fighting stance. She tapped twice and more options came up, then she selected the option below the one she had selected last time. Together the orange dots made up the image of three large cylinders. It intrigued me to see what this activity would be based on. "Are you able to tell me in advance what I will have to do?" I asked, despite already knowing the answer.

"If I did that, it would lose the element of surprise and you would have less training in being able to sense things before they happen."

"OK." I mumbled.

"Let's see how you do on this one."

I took a deep breath, knowing that I needed to be prepared

for anything. But, it was the basic settings.

It couldn't be that bad, could it?

When the course began, the same thing happened - the surrounding things faded away and left me engulfed in a darkness that I couldn't see in.

It was a few seconds before anything else happened. I was in a fighting stance when I saw the cylinder made up of orange dots, hurtling towards me.

I could dodge it, I thought, only I had a feeling that that wasn't what I was supposed to do. So instead I thought of the things I could do instead of dodging it: I could stand my ground and see what it would do, I could punch it or I could kick it. The moment came too soon, and I stood my ground with just my forearms crossed in front of my face to protect me from the potential impact; when it finally reached me, the force sent me flying back and I ended up having a hard landing on the floor, with the breath knocked out of my lungs. I started coughing and gasping for air, while tears accumulated in the corner of my eye.

However, soon after that impact, there came another cylinder, and now that I knew I couldn't stand my ground, I dodged it. Only then did I realise my mistake. When it was two inches away from me I saw a force beside it as well, a force that was only a little weaker than the actual cylinder itself - a force that sent me flying. At that point, I knew I would be covered in bruises by the time I finished the activity. When the next cylinder came flying towards me, I pushed all my strength into a punch which I made sure to throw right at its glowing centre. On impact, the most unexpected thing happened... it disintegrated. As soon as I punched it, the orange dots which made up the shape of the cylinder dissipated into thin air, and I was once again left in the darkness breathing heavily. If that's what it took to defeat the cylinders, then so be it. One by one, group after group, they came and I punched each one of them hard into their glowing centre. The cylinders felt rubbery and plastic, despite being made up of orange dots. It took a while, but I started to slow as my arms became tired from punching so many.

I learned that it took a certain force for them to disintegrate, and if I punched too lightly, it ended up still hitting me. Even though my body was obviously tiring, I refused to stop and pushed through the overwhelming urge to collapse from exhaustion.

"Can I..." Punch.

"Stop..." Punch.

"Now..." Punch. Punch. "Please," I asked desperately, despite not knowing if she could hear me or not. But it was confirmed that she could after the cylinders slowed down, and eventually, the remaining cylinders broke down into floating dots to form the shape of Crystiana. "Have you reached your limit, dear?" Whatever these orange dots were, they weren't just dots, but something else entirely.

"Yes..." The darkness engulfed me once again.

∼

WHEN I WOKE UP, I was back in my chambers, resting on the comfortable, floating platform. I groaned and stretched as I got up. I caught a whiff of myself and knew to head straight to the shower.

I frowned as I tried to remember how I had got here, but then realised that I had blacked out in the training chambers. By the looks of it, Crystiana had probably teleported me right to my bed, as I was still in my training suit. I got up quickly and froze in terror when I heard a voice. My heart caught in my throat until I was able to detect where the voice was coming from, "You have one new message from Crystiana". I sighed with relief as I realised who it was. "Oh hi, Nora."

"Hello, Margaret. Welcome back. Would you like to read the message?"

"Yes please." I watched as the screen display changed from the words Nora was saying, to a word written on a post-it in cursive handwriting. Nora started to speak again, "This post-it reads 'Meet me in the World chambers when you have freshened up. You will be having history next.' End of message."

"That's strange," I muttered. I had only had training sessions until now. I not expected to be learning about other things. However, as I thought it through, I realised that that was what Jake had meant by finding out everything soon enough. I smiled, I would finally get some answers, and I could ask her some of the hundreds of questions that had been swarming around in my head since I arrived in this world. I was about to think about the questions I should ask, when Nora interrupted my thoughts, "What do you find strange, Margaret?"

"Strange?" I recalled, "Oh. Oh nothing, I was just thinking about the message. Thank you for reading it to me Nora. You may turn off now."

"Shutting down."

"Wait!" I called out to her. She stopped and the smiley face returned back to the screen, "Yes, Margaret."

"Could you play some music… preferably inspired by forest sounds?"

"Sure."

I smiled in response, though I doubted she could see. The forest is what Jake and I had first been introduced to; it had been the start of our adventure. Soon enough, she started playing some soothing forest sounds, birds tweeting and the nearby waterfall. The music seemed to be coming from all areas of the room, making it seem like I was actually in a forest. "Suggestion. Would you like me to change the theme to the forest?"

"Good idea, Nora." I agreed. Instantly, I could see the windows behind the curtains become brighter. I ran to open them. Light streamed into my chambers as I looked into the crisp quality of a forest view.

"Wow… This is amazing." I got no response, but I don't think I would have paid attention if I had, as I was too busy trying to absorb the details of the clear sky and crystal-clear water. After seeing nothing but crystals and gemstones, wooden doors and polished floors, this felt like a dream. I had almost forgotten what it was like to look up at the sky. The view curved around me, making it feel like my chambers were on the verge of a river, placed right on the glistening pebbles. It looked and felt so real and I had a strong urge to wade into the water. A bird squawking jolted me out of my daze, and instantly the excitement of learning about my true origins came flooding back to me.

"I have to have a shower, and quickly." I quickly turned the temperature to hot; I needed hot water if I wanted to get some relief from my aching muscles. I breathed in the steam of the shower and started humming the soothing melody of the lullaby my mum had always sung to me...

I frowned as I remembered my mum's silver locket, which I had worn every day at the orphanage. I had taken it from her dresser the day they died. Tears welled up in my eyes as I realised what was happening; I was slowly forgetting her: her presence, what she looked like, what she sounded like. It had been almost five years now, and her features were starting to blur. Her warm, hazel eyes and pleasant laugh. Her great cooking and singing skills. They were all melding into each other to create a single blur of emotions and memories. My time with her had been cut too short, I sniffled the tears up my nose, hardly being able to breathe in the stifling hot air.

I stepped out of the shower, and combed and braided my hair into two. When I stepped out of the bathroom, the change in temperature was drastic. I inhaled the cool air as I listened to the soothing sounds of birds tweeting and water trickling, trying to calm my emotions. I headed to my closet and looked through the clothes for something comfortable. After searching through a few dark oak drawers filled with different jeans and tops, I finally picked an outfit consisting of a lilac crop top and a pair of black joggers. I slipped on some white socks along with a pair of black slip-on shoes.

I was about to head out of the chambers when I remembered the music was still playing, "You can stop the music now. Thank you, Nora."

The music faded away and I opened the heavy dark oak door to step into the glowing hallway.

"Time to get answers," I muttered to myself. Since I didn't have a clue where the World Chambers were, Crystiana had set the path so I only needed to walk down the hallway and turn a corner. I took a deep breath as I stood in front of yet another dark oak door.

CHAPTER 12

RED

After being inside rooms all day, I made the doors to the veranda swing open with a flick of my wrist. I needed air, even if it was still underground. I couldn't help but feel trapped in a cage where I was at the mercy of Madella; and that was exactly how she wanted me to feel. Instead, I focused on why I was here and how important it was that I found out as much as I could.

I looked down at the same bioluminescent river I had seen flowing under the bridge I walked on with Razel to come here. It stretched alongside the entire landscape and blurred into the distance.

I marvelled at the meticulous skill and power I imagined it took to control all the spells in the place. I could sense the different ones, as some had more of a distinguishable scent than others. I wondered if it was something only the magically inclined could sense, but appreciated it all the same.

The air outside the palace felt fresher but still carried the density that came with having so many spells hovering around in the air. They all blended into one sickeningly sweet scent, so strong you could almost taste it. I had thought going outside would make me feel better, but I was wrong, I could only feel her effect more.

I closed the doors behind me and flung off my shoes, observing the room properly for the first time. The lilac carpet felt soft under my feet and the teal walls added a soft touch to the room. The lights were off so the glowing crystals in the ceiling were bright. They glowed lime green and were a great comfort as I lay down on the queen-sized bed and snuggled into the silk sheets. I sighed and hopped into the bathroom that smelled mostly of roses and pear. It was a gentle reminder that I was still in the fae realm. There were no baths here, but an enchanted tub made of glazed leaves. It served as somewhere the water could through or stay in, depending on the spell you used. I peeled off my current clothes and used the spell written on papyrus to activate the alta flower. It could only have been sourced from Bellbon or Augustine. Just like the triphants, the fae also had an alternate system to the humans. They were more into bartering, making twisted deals that would most likely benefit them more than it did the other party.

I watched as the salmon-pink petals of the Alta extended from their shrunken state and the stigma poured chilled water onto my skin. I lathered a generous apple-scented soap onto myself for a long while. Eventually, I got out of the smooth tub that had grown soft because of the amount of water I had used.

Once I'd dried myself off, I shrugged on an olive nightgown made from diaphanous material and snuggled into the soft, sweet-smelling sheets. I succumbed to the darkness quickly and wished for the next day to come quickly.

My eyelids fluttered before fully opening. At first, I thought I'd somehow arrived back into my chambers, but the teal walls told me otherwise. I stretched briefly before hopping out of the warm sheets and headed into the bathroom to splash some cold water onto my face. It would wake me up fully and get me into the right frame of mind. I couldn't help but feel a wave of disappointment when I felt warm water trickle from the alta flower onto my face. I wiped my face with a dry sponge and sighed. I had forgotten the water was warm in the day and cold at night. I searched the drawer for a pair of pants and a top; the closest I could find was a plum skirt and crop top.

I had also forgotten about the extremities of fae clothing. For a female fae, you either covered everything or barely anything at all. Madella and Saphella wore body-hugging dresses, but that was their choice. I needed something I could fight in at a moment's notice.

Once I'd got dressed, I made my way out of my chambers, noticing glowing gold cursive handwriting on the cream-coloured door. It read 'Meet me in the Greenhouse.' I headed out of my chambers, and the concentrated smell of Madella's magic greeted me. I pushed it to the back of my mind and continued to the place I'd met her once before. Normally I would have teleported, but I needed to conserve my magic since she had a hold on my gemstone.

I wandered down the pellucid steps and hopped across the bioluminescent lake using the large boulders instead of the bridge. Once I was on the other side of the building, I retraced my steps until I reached the greenhouse, except it wasn't the greenhouse. I had somehow ended up at the lounge. The alden I'd seen when I first arrived, waddled up to me. "Madella ordered me to meet you here," it croaked, its voice gravelly and rough in its texture.

"Take me to the greenhouse, please... What's your name?" I asked.

"Walter," it grunted.

"Oh, right." It turned and walked off, not checking to see if I was following. Aldens had extensive hearing so they could pick up sounds from miles away. They were a great security measure to have around, especially in Madella's case. It walked quite fast for its pudgy build, but it was a good speed for me. The time passed by quickly; the tapestries on the walls I had previously paid keen attention to were nothing but blurs in my memory. We reached the same aluminium door Saphella had brought me to for the first time and the alden walked right through. I breathed in the mixture of aromas, then strolled in after the alden. I saw the gleaming whiteness of her lab coat and heard her saying, "You're here. Finally."

"Thanks for sending Walter."

"I wanted him to see if you were trustworthy. Now I can just write on your door wherever I want you to go."

"Transportation spell…"

"It's good you've heard of it." She turned to face Walter. "You can leave now Walter, goodbye."

He sped away mumbling things under his breath.

"I told you what I know about Reina, now you need to know what to use against her."

I nodded in response and she continued, "As you may already have figured out, Reina is the demon queen, and, as the queen, she had an heir who would follow her onto the throne. We know she is a triphant who married into demon blood so what we need will be things to weaken her control over demons; that is the only power she has over them. Once we figure that out then, of course, you know what weakens a triphant; combine the two and you should have your answer." She turned towards me. "I thought about what you said about the war and I know it will impact all of us. I've been working on potent protection and attacking spells against demons but I'll need to teach you what I know about them, and the fae history, not just the from triphants' point of view."

She showed me some of her books and her scribbles grew to make more and more sense as she explained herself further. The fae had come into contact with demons a few times in the last few centuries, especially on solstices.

After a period of giving me prompts about what the books were about, she left me with a long pile to go through. "Do you have a library I can go to?"

She took a sharp breath and pursed her lips. "Yes, I do."

"May I go?"

Her facial expression tightened before it loosened and she sighed.

"You may. I will have my daughter accompany you there." She wrote symbols in the air and they glowed in response to her magic. I recognised it as a calling symbol. A few seconds after it had dissipated, I sensed Saphella's presence near the greenhouse. My senses had grown stronger since having back my gemstone. Even though it was locked in the enchanted cage, I could still draw on part of its magic.

"Mother," Saphella announced.

"Saphella," she responded and I watched as her posture stiffened. "Do me a favour and take Red to the library."

She took a deep breath. "Sure." She snapped her fingers and I was outside the greenhouse. I watched as the door shut with a slam. Saphella sighed and walked off, expecting me to follow her.

"Can you teleport like your mother?" I asked.

"No. I am forbidden from it," she replied

We were entering a darker part of the palace and the ground began responding to our footsteps, glowing a bright colour with every step we took. We climbed a set of spiral steps for what seemed like the longest while.

Saphella broke the silence by saying, "You will not find a library like this anywhere else. I think you'll love it though."

At the top of the stairs, there was a deathly drop to the ground. An elevated platform hovering in the middle served to be the only way to get to the other side. She hopped onto the platform gracefully, almost as if it were second nature.

It held its position and I followed her onto it. She used her magic to move it along and we stepped off once it reached the other side.

There were thick grey doors that towered over us, but a gentle push was all it took for them to open.

"Welcome to my library - my safe haven. The only place my mother can't hear or see me," she announced as I took in the multi-storey shelves filled with innumerable books, some that glistened and some that glowed. There was a sweet, musty smell that welcomed me inside. Scattered across the shelves were coruscant gold ladders that stretched all the way to the top.

In the corners, there were resplendent, olive green desks and underneath was a wooden floor that was so shiny it might as well be a mirror. I looked up and the far ceiling was decorated with putti and majestic naked women of various skin colours.

There were midnight blue ceramic pillars patterned with stars; they were a sharp contrast from the surrounding cream walls.

After giving me a while to take in the spectacular setting, she asked, "What type of books do you like?"

"I'm mostly into non-fiction books, ones that can help me learn new things, but I'll never turn down a good romance."

"Well I guarantee you we have a lot of those," she giggled.

I smiled and suggested, "Do you happen to have any on the demon race?"

She grimaced before answering, "Quite a few, but the ones I've read are all made up of mostly guesses; then again, no one's really been to the demon realm, much less been committed enough to write about it."

"Hm... I've been there."

Her upturned eyes widened. "Really?"

I nodded. "It was part of a mission, but trust me when I say it's not a pleasant place." I sighed and continued, "I understand what you're saying though. I expected them to be mostly guesses, but I want to see which guesses align with what I already know; hopefully I can figure something out. My aim is to see the bigger picture to all this- there always is."

"Follow me," she said.

She led the way past various piles of books stacked in random places, along the way we passed service elves. Some she introduced me to and others she simply greeted as they were all busy doing activities.

Saphella seemed a more exuberant individual when she wasn't under the constant watch of her mother, especially when it came to showing off her interests. On the way, she explained why the books were set up in the way that they were. The ones she thought more interesting were moved to the bottom and the ones she thought boring were moved to the top. She told me where the fantasy books were, the romance books and the sci-fi.

"Oh, and I think you'll adore this one."

She pulled a light red book out from the bottom of the romance section and handed it to me. The light in the library faded as we went towards the back, but there were dim lamps set up to illuminate the books. I watched as she trailed her index finger across the titles and selected a few from a shelf, then a particularly chunky one from a pile. It had a lock on it.

"I think these should have something useful in them."

She turned to me and said, "My mother told me you had telekinesis. Could you use it to carry the books?"

I nodded and swirled my wrist, my red magic circling the books and carrying them along behind us.

"Whoa..." she murmured and I grinned to myself. I'd always loved validation growing up, something that had never left me.

We sat down at one of the desks and I heard her mutter, "What else haven't I shown her..." Then she said, "Would you like to see the ceiling when it's opened up?"

"Sure."

She wrote symbols in the air which darkened the area so that when the ceiling opened, the glow of the sky covered the library in a mystical shade of blue. I let out a gasp as indigo, lilac and fuchsia mixed to create an ethereal canvas in the starry sky.

"Wow," I whispered.

"Yeah..." Her voice was tinged with melancholy. "When I get out of here, I want to explore the world. There's more for me out there, I can feel it. The old witch can't lock me up forever."

I heard hints of hatred in her words but didn't want to get into it. "I'm assuming you have a plan."

She nodded. "Over the years, I learned to read comfort books out of the library and informative ones inside. It keeps the paranoia down. She sees everything and hears everything, Red. With the information from the few books she left about the fae realm and the knowledge I have of the palace, I think I can escape."

I pursed my lips. It seemed she knew what she was doing – but escaping was always much easier in one's head than it was to carry out.

I opened my mouth to say something when she blurted, "Having one of the most renowned, powerful witches as your mother is very much a curse rather than a blessing."

I sighed. "I can only imagine, but… as long as you know what you're doing," I concluded; and that was that.

I was about halfway into a book about the demon realm creatures when she asked, "What do you and my mother talk about?"

"Demons."

"I was hoping for more info than that but the point is that…" She paused for a bit then continued, "I want to help."

I scowled. "I'm trying to figure out what to do so I can figure out how to help."

"So then let me do the same."

"Huh?"

She put down her romance and said, "Let me help you figure out how to help."

I sighed. "It's more than that. I know information dating back centuries. These books won't be of any use to you, only me."

I returned my attention to my book.

"So that's it then? I'm just gonna watch as you do it yourself?"

"You…" I paused and thought about it carefully before I continued, "Actually… I think there may be something you can help me with."

She smirked. "I knew it."

I explained the situation with Razel to her and she grew tenser as time passed. "You think when Reina came... she turned him to her side?" She asked.

"I suspect but I can't be sure. I still need some sort of proof."

"I'll look into it," she muttered before returning to her book.

"Thank you."

After finishing one, I moved onto the next - written in Madella's scribbles. It gave me an idea of what her grimoire was like. Remembering what I read was never a problem for me, but as soon as the words started jumbling together I knew I would not make any more headway. From instinct, I reached for magic from my gemstone but felt the jolting pain from the enchanted cage. I scowled internally and turned to see a sleeping Saphella.

I wasn't sure when she'd fallen asleep, but the sky had turned black so I figured we'd been there a while. I had no idea where her chambers were but I thought I would do her a favour and carry her down the steps with my telekinesis. I grabbed the rest of the books and headed out of the library for the day, the heavy doors shutting softly behind me with a click. Going down the steps took half the time it had taken to climb up and it wasn't long before I was nudging her awake.

Once again the floor responded to my steps by glowing various colours; as soon as I was out of the dark area leading to the staircase, I placed her on the first bench I found. Her eyelids fluttered open and she looked around, probably disoriented. She sat up fast and her plait of auburn hair swung around before finally settling down. Her eyebrows furrowed; I interpreted her puzzled expression as meaning, "How did I get down here?"

"I used my telekinesis to bring you down the steps."

"Oh… Thank you."

I smiled in response and rose up. She stood up as well and towered over me by two inches. "I wish you a good night, Red."

"Same to you." Her basil green, long skirt swished from side to side as she sauntered into the distance. I turned in the opposite direction and went to my chambers.

CHAPTER 13

PINK

I had just mustered up the courage to knock, when the door automatically opened, "Welcome Margaret. Do have a seat." Crystiana greeted from the back of the dim-lit room.

I followed her voice and sat facing her. It only took me a short while to get accustomed to the dim lighting, and I studied the few visible details. After seeing the many books that were set on wooden shelves, I realised that we were in a library that was filled to the brim with books. There were many shelves stacked beside each other, leaving little room to walk, and each stretched to heights I couldn't see.

I could read them in my spare time.

"Wow…" I muttered and then paid attention to Crystiana, who was in front of me.

We were separated by a transparent table, lightly tinted with blue. I gulped the urge to cry, as the blue was a miserable reminder of Jake. I wiped away the tears welling up in my eyes, sniffed and focused on what she was saying instead of Jake's disappearance. "In today's history lesson, you will be learning about how triphants were created."

I pondered, "And I can ask as many questions as I like?"

"I would prefer it if you waited until the end. But yes… You can."

I grinned, "OK." If only she knew how much I yearned for answers.

She started the lesson, telling the story of how the triphants species came about. "At the beginning of creation, the Founding Father made the earth as the garden planet, along with mankind and all other living things on earth, whether they were magical or non-magical. In protection over his creation, he created the three Time Gods to watch over the life and ensure that fate was not intervened with. These gods were called Past, Present and Future. Although they were given duties in supervision, they could only do so in their time dimension. Furthermore, they were each gifted with special abilities, Past took what was meant to go, Future brought into the world and Present made sure that nothing was out of place and that balance remained. Since they could not leave their dimensions, they wanted a pair of eyes and ears which they could depend on to act immediately and not cause catastrophic damage. They needed something discreet and powerful. To answer this need, they created triphants.

This was a species that possessed the ability to time travel, a direct connection to the time gods' powers, embedded in our blood. However, as time went on and triphants evolved, some had weaker connections than others. This is how family planning started and, you could say, forced marriages. Triphants had their children bond into powerful bloodlines to create stronger, more complex ones. That is how we have powerful families who are well known in the triphant world, and are typically given automatic respect and an easy, privileged life on a silver platter."

"It's interesting to hear about other species from triphants, humans and demons. Also, Grammie. I would like to know the truth."

"About what, dear?" She responded calmly.

"About me, about our family. I just want to know the truth."

"Well."

"Please," I begged.

She sighed, "You have a right to know the truth. So, I shall tell you." She took a deep breath before continuing, "Our family line is quite short, but so far, we have carried down the line of pinks. I am the daughter of the first pink, Phillipia Dagon. Though the mortality of triphants is extended, not endless, this realm preserves age so we are able to live longer than others. For this reason, I have known and outlived many of the chosen."

"How old are you?"

"Old."

I sighed. "OK. Continue."

"The line chosen for pink has been short and that's my fault."

"Why?" I asked though I hated myself for interrupting her.

"Well… as a chosen triphant, before you are sent back to Earth from Clorista, you have two choices. You can either continue with the power you have, dedicating it to protecting your gemstone or you can give up your power and lead a life on Earth as if you were a human."

"OK."

"But as Pink, you have an extra option. To become the next trainer for the chosen triphants. You would have knowledge passed on to you so you would know what to do and what not to do, and the realm of secrets would be passed on to your power."

"And why do only pinks have this power?"

"Because we can control every triphant gemstone existing. We possess the most power and thus attract more evil. But if we stay in Clorista, the threat of luring malicious beings into the human realm is less likely. It makes it easier for the rest."

"Why do we have to be so selfless?" I muttered.

"Well… Your mother understood this and severed her link to the pink gemstone to live a life as a human. Only, the power she gave up ended up being passed down to you." My eyes widened. "She tried to protect you for the longest while, Margaret. But when her leftover magic ran out, and she could no longer use charms to conceal her location, it happened to be on your ninth birthday."

"And…"

"And one of the elders found her… and banished her."

I didn't know what emotion I felt at that moment, but tears pricked my eyes as I asked, "So… she's alive?" It sounded so crazy I immediately rejected the possibility, not wanting to get my hopes up.

"Yes," she admitted.

I spat, "You knew?" I looked at her with an expression of disbelief; the feeling of betrayal weighed heavy on my heart. "I can't believe this." I whispered incredulously, "Anything else I should know?" I angrily wiped a tear from my eye, too angry and puzzled to care about my tone.

Crystiana sighed and snapped her fingers. I jumped and then frowned when I saw a brown cardboard box wrapped in a light pink ribbon appear in front of me. "What's that?"

"It was the gift your mother was going to give to you on your ninth birthday. She wanted to tell you the truth."

I studied it carefully and recognised symbols of the triphant language that were carved into it. If I had seen this as my nine-year-old self, I would have thought nothing of them except for them being pretty symbols, just part of the design. I traced the lines carefully and tried to ignore the tears that were threatening to flow, creating kaleidoscopes in my vision. I quickly wiped them away and opened the box.

Inside was a shiny, silver locket. It also had triphant symbols engraved into it. When I pressed it, it clicked open and I saw a picture of me as a baby and another picture beside it, a picture of my birthmark glowing. "My birthmark..."

"Your birthmark is a scar, a scar from being chosen."

"Oh..." All the pieces were quickly clicking together, like a puzzle.

The anger oozed away from me steadily. "Could you... could you read what it says on the box and the locket?" She snapped her fingers and the box teleported to her. "Let's see... Beautiful.

Blessed. Cursed. Powerful. Unique," she read from the box, then she swiftly took up the locket, and read, "To Adira."

Adira? "Who's that?"

"That's... You."

Me? "How can that be me, my name is... Adira... My name is Adira. "Adira..." I whispered to myself, wondering why it sounded so familiar and foreign at the same time.

"Ameliora... Now I see what you've done." I heard Crystiana whisper as she smiled while holding a note.

"What?" The box appeared in front of me, along with the note. "Read the note, dear." So I did just that and saw what she meant.

> Dear Sweet Adira,
> Happy Birthday my sweet child. If you happen to get this before your birthday, then here is the warning that you may experience slight discomfort as the rest of your power returns. This spell has suppressed your true self and your true powers, until now. I hope you will learn to forgive me and know that all is not lost. If I'm not there with you then, whatever happened to me was not because of you, it was because of my mistakes. I have left you with clues as to how to find me, and, when you do, I hope you have learned and grown into your power. I hope you have fought for the greater good and that you have found your own meaning in this life. I'm

sorry that you too were cursed with this responsibility and blessed with the power. But no matter what happens, I love you, my sweet Adira.

 Never forget that.
 Much love,
 From Mum

Tiny gasps came, then soon my body was racked with sobs. My heart throbbed, yearning for her as my nose became hot and stuffy.

No matter how much I seemed to wipe them from my eyes, the tears continued to flow; I could taste the salt as they trickled onto my lips. Waves of overwhelming emotions hit me as if I had seen her die all over again, and it was a while before I could numb it down to one emotion - wistfulness.

I missed her.

I missed her, and I missed Dad.

I missed her voice, her warmth, her personality.

I missed her presence in my life.

Reading that note had given me a taste of something I had been deprived of for too long and from too early. It was reading the note, knowing that she was gone and the budding hope of being able to find her again that was making me feel this way.

I felt a warmth beside me and a gentle hand brought me towards her chest.

Family, she was family.

I cried and cried; I cried until I had no tears left, and all that was left was the feeling of numbness.

Late that night, I was lying in bed, drifting in and out of consciousness, contemplating what the note had said. For those few moments, I felt her warmth, I felt her presence, and I felt her. As I revelled in her words, I finally drifted off into an uneasy sleep.

CHAPTER 14

RED

I slipped on some lime loose-fitting pants and a crocheted crop top. There was no note on my door this time, but when I opened it, I stepped straight into the greenhouse. Madella was stirring a bubbling, orange concoction in the stripping, black cauldron.

"Finally you're here. I was about to send Walter to retrieve you," she started.

"Sorry about that."

"I was working on a specific type of potion. Do you have the book I gave you?"

Oh right, the book.

"Oh, uhm…" I looked around, only to see a grey wall. The door to my chambers had disappeared. She sighed and snapped her fingers. The book appeared on the green-tinted clear desk beside her. It flicked to a page somewhere in the middle and settled when she pressed her finger to the text.

"Right here. I need you to read through it, you'll get a basic understanding of how it works and the ingredients needed to make it." I skimmed through the scribbles as she continued, "From what I've learned about the previous Reds, you're supposed to have the most refined photographic memory out of all the chosen."

"That's true."

"You could have finished the entire book yesterday. Why didn't you?"

"My attention was split between many things."

"Like what?"

"Books on the demon realm. I was trying to piece together things about them from another species' perspective."

"Any luck?" she asked as turned to look at me.

I sighed. "So far, it's only the obvious facts about the demon realm. They've given the creatures their own name. Tragedors are named Navsbors, protectors of the demon realm barrier. I know they circle around each entry, but that can be solved with mercury powder."

"Mercury powder will not pass this time. It will suggest that you are one of them but you will still look like a foreigner. You need something more like…"

I had just read the page she gave me and finished for her, "Invisibility."

"Exactly…" She lifted a tube out of the cauldron filled halfway with the orange liquid. "Try some."

I reached for it then hesitated. Her eyes darkened and she exhaled, "If you think I've wasted so much time waiting to poison you, then you are terribly mistaken."

"Right I am." The colour of the potion was pure, without the murky look of dark magic. I took the tube and drank it. It tasted sour but had a sweet aftertaste. I set the tube down on the table and a few seconds after ingesting it, I looked at my hands to see them fading. Soon, I could see the tiled stone floor underneath as though I was looking through water. After just a few seconds, I could no longer see my ivory skin tone, but I could see everything around me. It was disorienting to look down and only see my crop top and pants.

I gasped. I could see my crop top and pants. "We'd have to go naked," I blurted.

"Not necessarily. The more you take, the more the invisibility spreads."

"What about a pairing spell for seeing beyond the invisibility?"

"Ah… You see, normally that wouldn't be possible, but you have the green gemstone on your side."

"Antimagic…"

"Exactly."

I had never fully considered Green. I'd been aware of their existence of course, but never really paid attention to their abilities. I focused mostly on perfecting the ones I had myself.

Antimagic.

It was an intriguing concept. A type of magic that was able to undo or oppose any spell. "I'll also be needing something for stamina. Interrealm portals take a lot of energy and I'll need a lot if I'm to fight Reina."

"Mm." Madella waved her hand; the book flipped its pages to another recipe. "This one works well for an energy booster. Every time you consume one, it should give you enough adrenaline for about ten minutes. But be careful, Red, by taking too much, you risk not being able to fight at all." Her face grew grim.

"I understand," I replied. She gave me an antidote potion so I could see myself again, before leading me through exactly how to make it. After that, she instructed me to do the exact same thing.

I prepared the materials the way she'd shown me and never once felt her gaze leave me. The mixture had reached the same tiger-orange colour I'd seen when I'd first entered. I poured some into a tube using a ladle and gave some to Madella to judge. After tasting some and tightening her face, she muttered, "Too much azvern, again."

I grew agitated. "But, you saw me add the azvern and didn't say anything."

"That's because I wanted to see how you did everything else. Interrupting making a potion too many times causes stress on a witch's magic and that never helps."

She was right. I sighed, used a vanishing spell on the potion and started again.

I couldn't recall how many times I had done it, but it was enough times for sweat beads to be trickling down my forehead and for my hands to be shaking. I sighed as I handed her the tube. Hopefully, this would be the last time.

She took the tube to her lips as usual and took a gulp. She paused and nodded in approval. "Perfect."

"Thank the gods," I said.

"Take some in a canister and use some of the preserving drops. I recommend going to the library. Do some more research."

I nodded. She snapped her fingers and my mess disappeared, returning her working station to the meticulous state it had been before.

Once I'd stored the invisibility potion away in a cupboard, I headed to the library. When I pushed the doors open, I saw Saphella reading the same romance novel. She'd made significant progress since the day before as she was nearly finished. "Hey," I said. The exhaustion had hit me hard, and I was met with a stinging pain from trying to pry some magic from my gemstone.

"Hey. I found some more books for you to read," she said without looking up from her book. My eyes skimmed the desk to find a small pile of books.

"Ah, thank you."

"My mother really did a number on you, didn't she?" she asked, giving me a knowing look.

"Yeah," I murmured, giving her a wry smile.

"You'll get used to it," she assured me.

I sighed and sat down to read 100 more stories. I desperately hoped this would all be worth it in the end.

CHAPTER 15

PINK

I dreamt of many things, but it didn't take me long to realise that they weren't just dreams - but memories. Though I had no recollection of them, they clicked right into place, as if filling in the blanks in my mind.

As it turned out, my mum did tell me everything- whether by stories or songs- but she glamoured it with her magic, so I wouldn't remember. In secret, she always called me Adira, she even spoke the triphant language when we were alone - that's why I knew how to speak it. She never dared write it down though as that made it harder to erase.

~

WHEN I WOKE UP, I was greeted by the same beams of light streaming through my curtains. The refulgent, yellow ball hovering just beyond the thick, transparent windows stayed consistent.

I had no motivation to get out of bed so I lay there and stared at the white ceiling.

At first, it looked smooth, but if you looked closely, you could see the designs etched into it. You could see the way the lines were all interconnected and flowed from one design to another.

After a while, I had mustered enough strength to roll out of bed, one limb at a time. I realised I had grown quite weak. But that didn't stop me from starting my usual routine of having a shower, combing and braiding my hair into two, and then heading to the closet to pick out an outfit.

I was just going through the training suits when I felt an unexpected sensation, hunger. I clutched my stomach as I felt the hot, ravenous sensation gnaw at me. I could barely recall the last time I had felt the urge to eat, except when I had just arrived. It turns out Jake was right; our bodies did work in a different way, even if I hadn't realised it at first. I needed food in my system and fast. My energy was draining by the second.

Why didn't Crystiana tell me about this?

I made a mental note to eat more often, even if I didn't feel like it. Anything to escape the pain of hunger.

I threw something on and hurried to the dining chambers. I ordered a spicy omelette, bacon and a plate full of cheese and ham sandwiches from the holographic menu. I frowned as I took the first bite of the sandwich. Eating had almost become a foreign feeling. I had to get used to swallowing and chewing all over again. I started eating the omelette before I remembered to use cutlery. I groaned in response to the satisfying crispiness of the bacon.

"I thought I'd find you here." I jumped as the voice echoed through the dining chambers. It was her. She strolled in with a flowing white dress. It seemed to glow in the golden hue of the chandeliers.

"I was wondering how long it would take for your system to need food," she started.

"How long did I go without it?"

"Well, if we were relating to Earth days, I would say about… three."

My eyes widened. "Three…" I muttered while taking the last of the cheese and ham sandwiches.

I was about to order another platter when she said, "You don't mind if I join you, do you?"

"No, not at all," I muttered, with my mouth full of cheese and ham. It was so long since I'd eaten, that I had forgotten my manners.

I selected a platter of toasted cheese sandwiches and my mouth watered as it appeared hot and steaming in front of me. My heart fluttered as I bit into the soft, melted cheese and the toasted bread crunched in my mouth. After that, I couldn't help but order seafood: lobsters, shrimp, and crabs with a generous helping of rice.

I finished it all off with a nice hot soup.

"Maybe you should eat more often, Adira," she remarked,

using her propped-up hands as a stand for her head to lean on. I froze.

Adira...

Adira... My name was Adira and that's what it had always been... Adira Dagon was who I was.

"Maybe..." I murmured, still in a trance.

Once I had eaten and my stomach felt bloated, I followed Crystiana to the training chambers. By the time we reached it, I started to feel the strength return to me. I never realised how good it felt to eat food; I felt complete.

"In today's training session, you will be focusing on using your magic."

My eyes lit up.

"You will learn exercises to help develop your knowledge of your powers, and learn to use it as second nature."

I nodded, determined to do my best in this lesson - to become stronger. I wanted to leave the shell of my old self behind as much as I could.

I expected her to bring up the holographic orange dots to start on another course; instead, she said, "As a fellow pink, I would know the best exercises to do since I spent many years studying my own power."

"Wait," I said, "I wanted to know how our gemstones work. Why do we need to carry them with us if we can use our powers without them?"

She smiled. "Well, believe it or not, you channel your power from your gemstone. Without it, you are simply using up the dregs left over in your body. Think of your gemstone as your power source… or one could refer to it as a battery charger. When you have it with you, it gives you a continuous flow of power."

"Oh… I understand now. And what you're saying is that without it I'm weak."

"Not exactly. Without your gemstone, you are simply just a vessel holding its power, but with it, you and your gemstone become one and you have an endless supply of its power. That's also why I'm training you, to give you an experience of what it's like without your gemstone. With your gemstone giving you constant power, it's almost as if it's spoon-feeding you, and you start to produce raw, unrefined power, and what use is that if you have no control over it?"

That question remained in my mind for the rest of the training session as she guided me through the swirls and embers of pink magic I could produce from my palm.

The many breathing exercises and muscle motions were a pain at first, but I got used to them after a while. I was yawning by the end of the session, and my entire body ached.

"How do you feel?" she asked.

"My muscles ache, but I feel quite refreshed."

She smiled, "Your power is like a pet. You need to train it if you want it to follow your every command."

It resonated with me when she dismissed me to get ready for our next session, History. I had a reassuring feeling that I would soon settle into a routine with Crystiana and finally be comfortable enough to call this place home.

The triphant history made the history of humans seem as if

they were clueless or small-minded, as they were ignorant of how the world truly came about. But Crystiana only went into how triphants were made, not how the chosen came about, or even the gemstones.

Why were the gemstones created?

I figured the history lesson was the perfect time to ask her.

Later that day, I settled into a steamy bath; its warmth massaged my aching muscles. I loved the soothing scent of the lavender and honey bath salts. I nearly fell asleep but managed to get out and dry myself off with haste. She said I could take as long as I wished, but I still didn't want to take too long. I picked out a flowery crop top with sleeves, along with black jeggings, then hurried off to the place I knew as the World Chambers.

As soon as I stepped close to the door, it opened automatically, courtesy of Crystiana. I strolled into the room and recognised the pillars of books: layers upon layers tucked tightly together. The room was brighter this time, from the light coming from the sheer curtains. It looked like the same ball of light that illuminated my bedroom. As I scanned the room I spotted Crystiana looking at a navy blue book in the left far corner of the library. "

Welcome, Adira," she said, "Do have a seat." I headed to the clear table, pulled out a metal chair and sat on the cushioned seat.

"Today you'll learn about The Founding War."

I nodded, already intrigued by the name. Crystiana put her hand about an inch above the clear, tinted table - more specifically, above a black circle engraved with silver triphant symbols.

It glowed a bright pink when she hovered her hand over it and spoke a word of the triphant language. The circle spun, growing faster each second and began to showcase a plethora of images. They went by in a flash and I was only able to get a glimpse of some; from the way the people in them dressed and the way they carried themselves, they seemed to be images from the past. Soon, the images stopped and we were left in a field of black roses.

"The Founding War happened here over 3,000 years ago," she said. "This is the product of darkness. All of these roses were stained black by the immense evil that once roamed this earth, one that threatens to roam again." I shivered and the image changed from the stained roses to a plain landscape with luscious green grass swaying in the wind. The air was sparkling with some kind of magic. "This is a view of the earth when all species lived in peace and harmony. This was before darkness reigned and the magical beings were forced to go into different realms - away from humans."

The images flickered to present three glowing wisps of magic.

"The first beings the Founding Father made were the time gods. This was to keep time flowing in an orderly manner. However, there are places where time doesn't apply and simply does not exist. The Milky Way is one of the galaxies the time gods control. They are the reason why it has evolved so much and has been free from chaos." The image changed to space, with several planets revolving around the sun.

"Humans were the first species to be granted full intelligence and triphants were a derivative of them; that is why we have the same build as them."

"That makes sense," I said, fascinated by the way the holographic dots worked.

"I'm glad, but bear in mind I have told you all of this so you will be able to understand what I'm about to tell you." I watched as the dots changed to a scene of magical creatures marching toward each other. The different shades and colours of magic in the air intertwined and swirled around one another. Most of the creatures had a grimace – all except one, who looked as if he were mocking them. His grey, lifeless face was streaked with purple veins and his eyes gave me an insight into the bottomless pits of hell.

"Who is that?" I asked.

As soon as I asked, she knew who I was talking about. The image zoomed in to spotlight him.

"That is the Dark Lord. No one knows his actual name. He is the controller of darkness. He cannot be destroyed, but he can be contained. He has been contained for the last few millennia since the Founding War. He's one of the greatest masterminds ever known. The conflict among the species only fuelled his power and gave him more control over us. That is when we realised that the only way we could ever defeat him was by weakening his power. We had to forgive one another in order to defeat this great evil. Great portions of each species had already been turned against their own sides so the odds against us were high."

It was hard to take this all in, but I listened intently as she continued, "The feud between faeries and humans had already gone too far to fix in the time we had. However, the triphants pooled their power to fuel the chosen Green triphant. We were able to reverse time just enough to help the chosen Red triphant to create dimensions and the Yellow triphant to influence the humans to work with the faeries for at least a while. With this collective power, we were able to unite and defeat the Dark Lord once and for all."

"Wow."

"But it is important to know how the war started, Adira."

I nodded. "OK, Grammie."

She smiled and continued, "There are four magical species in this world. The witches, faeries, demons and dragons. In the beginning, we all lived in peace and harmony, all serving our purpose on the earth and maintaining balance. This was until darkness found a way to infiltrate the world we had so carefully built and developed to fit for each species."

"Even the demons?"

"Yes, even them. But, we'll get to that part. At that time, demons were… They were humans."

My eyes widened and my heart caught in my throat.

"How is that possible?"

"Each magical species had certain mental barriers that prevented them from being so susceptible to the mind control of the Dark Lord. Their brains are so weak and malleable that once they are taken control of… That's all it takes for them to turn to evil. It was subtle at first. He created toxic traits such as greed, manipulation, and the desire to be in control despite their powerless states. The only ones who really overcame it were the children with the blood of a magical species."

"So the whole human race... became... demons."

"Most... At first, it was just their mental state and most fought it... It was called the craze, they went after one another, wanting to control one another until groups united and wanted to take control of other species. The humans were a great race at first, but they soon proved to be a nuisance to any magical being out there. That's how the dragons and faeries turned against them. Those of us who carried the same mentality as those humans were called dark triphants. But, the main reason why triphants were created..."

"Was to keep the balance."

She nodded emphatically. "Yes. At this point, even the other magical races had turned against us for trying to help the humans... but it was clear after a while that there was nothing we could do – nothing except face the enemy head-on. That was the one thing all species were able to agree on. Get rid of the nuisance once and for all." The image flickered from naked humans fighting and progressively turned into an image of other creatures.

"The more humans succumbed to the darkness threatening to take over, the more they were transformed into the horrible beings you now see as demons."

I shivered once again as the image changed to oversized gargoyles with black papery skin - some had even grown talons. Though I couldn't feel the evil, it was clear from the black auras of evil around them, eating away at their consciences. Most importantly, streaks of purple had replaced their veins and contaminated their blood.

The mark of the Dark Lord. An unexpected rage developed in me. "All those lives..."

"Gone. Just like that."

Tears of rage pricked my eyes. I wiped them away harshly and demanded, "Tell me the rest. I have to know."

"When we realised that humans were being controlled by an invisible force, we came together to form a plan. The chosen triphants used their direct link to the time gods to communicate the wisest options for how to deal with the situation. We worked hard to drastically develop our forces to their highest standard and for an extended period of time. However… it was a while before we were finally able to gain the trust of the other species. We worked in secret, away from the humans. Until one day, word came from a Diablum - the name we gave to those humans who had already fully transformed. It gave us a date - the date on which the fate of all the magical species and the survival of the human race would be dictated. From the same message, we also learned the name of our nefarious enemy. This date was the day of the confrontation - the day on which we would see the Dark Lord himself."

"Was the confrontation the image I saw the Dark Lord in?"

"Yes." She made a swirly gesture with her index finger that changed what we were seeing to the moving picture of the magical forces swirling and repelling from one another. "Once we learned exactly who - or what - we would be going up against, we needed the strength of all of our strongest forces.

For us, it couldn't just be the chosen; also had to include people without the universe stone power. The Elite warriors were developed, as we were recruiting other Triphants who had developed special abilities. Some say it was a gift from the time gods to help us adapt to our surroundings - a form of evolution. But whatever it was, it was exactly what we needed, or so we thought."

"What does that mean?" I asked, frowning.

"Well, nothing mattered as long as there was conflict. People had had families that were humans, and the half-humans were despised for the damage they were doing to the earth. When confrontation day had come, most of the fairies and dragons had teamed up as anti-human teams fighting with the Triphants but only because we all had the same agenda. For the most part, we defeated his forces; but we realised that he was not weakening. And the rest you know; we figured out that the Dark Lord fed on darkness and evil and conflict and we stopped every conflict we had. The first Red sealed each magical species and the chosen triphants into a realm. The triphants' realm was connected to human realm to protect them, something we had sworn to do."

"So that day is the day when everything changed. The confrontation."

"Indeed. Now the humans that exist all have traces of magical blood. That's why some humans, like Red, possess the ability to wield a universe stone."

"Oh." It had never occurred to me that Red wasn't born into the triphant world. "That's... interesting."

"Only the pink bloodline is hereditary, or so I believe."

"Why do you say…?"

"It's okay, Adira. I'm sure it's nothing."

"Yes, but you could still tell me."

"It really has no significance whatsoever, it's just a theory that I haven't concluded yet."

"No!" My fist slammed onto the table and she gasped. "Sorry, I just don't care. I still need to know." My gaze didn't falter as she stared at me with uncertainty.

She sighed. "One of the chosen triphants - Yellow to be specific. – he had a child with a human, who fell prey to the Dark lord's influence during her pregnancy. I think somehow - his powers got passed on to the child. I think the child used these abilities to become the demon king. It also means that Jake could be a member of the chosen too."

My eyes widened. "But, how? Aren't there only four universe stones?"

"On Earth."

"There's more?"

"Yes, but they can only be used by a Triphant, or the person chosen."

"Oh…"

"Yes, and since Jake is half triphant… who knows? Anything is possible."

"You're right…"

"But, that's it for today's history lesson. You should rest up."

I pondered for a while. "Is there another room I can go in besides my chambers?"

"Actually... There is." She stood and snapped her fingers. We appeared in front of another steep dark oak wood door with no knob. "I'll make it so only you can access it. Just press your hand to the door and you can walk right in."

I pressed my hand to the door and it glowed pink around the outline of it. I had expected it to be solid, but after a moment, it became invisible and I stumbled in.

It was dark except for the light coming from the luminous trickling stream on the side of a wall, and some candescent gemstones embedded into the stone, glimmering off its light. The air was still, yet pulsing with life. The colours that danced around the room were vibrant. and each gave off its own aura. I felt a sense of peace. The temperature was comfortable, with revitalising coolness coming from the mini luminescent stream. "Thank you, Crystiana."

"Of course. Your mother had one just like this," she said from beyond the door. I could sense her presence leaving a few seconds after that, and that's when I truly felt alone and at peace. This room made me feel safe. I knew it would protect me if anything were to happen. In a way, it made me feel more whole than my chambers. I liked the fact that I could request something from Grammie and she would understand exactly what I needed, I liked the fact that she understood me. I was getting more and more comfortable in Clorista; it felt like the home I had longed for ever since my parents died... Or at least my dad.

Even though the hope of finding my mother had ignited a fire in me, the disappointment of never being able to see him again still weighed my heart down. All I could hope for was that the things she had said gave me the clues I needed to find her. I trailed my fingertips along with the chilled, aquamarine tiles and watched as each responded, with their turquoise tone glowing brighter.

I strolled over to a patch with no tiles where there was a fuzzy material. It held its form as I sat cross-legged on it and imagined a peaceful setting where it was just me in an undisturbed meadow of dancing grass and crystal clear water – a place where the air glittered with magic and the world was colourful instead of grey. In this place, I felt truly at peace; it was my subconscious home.

After a while of being there, I went to soak in a warming bath full of pale pink petals. After having a brief conversation with Nora, I turned off the lights and drifted into comfortable darkness.

When I woke up, I followed the same routine and reached the training chambers just as Crystiana strode in, with the familiar sound of her heels echoing in the large space. "Hello, dear," she said.

"Hello."

She snapped her fingers and a crystal glass full of crystal water appeared, hovering in front of me. "Drink that. Your time away from your gemstone will have weakened your magic and today you will be using it. The crystal water will act as a temporary booster until the time when you receive it." I took the cup and sipped at it as she continued: "Today you will be focusing on your accuracy with your magic."

She snapped her fingers once again and the square device she used to control the holographic training system materialised in front of her. "For this, you will be in a basic training mode, but don't be surprised if it switches on you. If I see it is becoming too easy for you, the setting will change to a false reality. However, the consequences remain the same. If you allow an obstacle to get past your barrier and touch you, it will hurt, and the pain will be real."

I shivered at the thought of it, but I suppose pain was a guaranteed way of making sure I didn't get distracted. I gulped down the rest of the silky sweetness; she waved her hand and it disappeared. She tapped a few times on the device and the orange dots exploded into the room once again, arranging themselves into the different courses available. She tapped on one with meteors as the image and I watched as the place grew darker. I adjusted to the darkness once again and mentally prepared myself for the course to start. I heard Crystiana's voice echo as she said, "Remember to stay focused at all times. You're going to hear things that are meant to distract you, but your goal is to destroy the obstacles; is that understood?"

"Yes, Grammie," I replied as I heard the whirring noises of a machine starting. As I got into my fighting stance, I realised that calling her Grammie had become more natural. I hadn't even thought about it as I said it.

When I saw the first orange obstacle in the distance, I got flashbacks to the first drill. I cringed at how out of shape I had been back then. In this drill, all I had to do was hit the obstacles with my magic. The crystal water was making my body simmer with my magic. I relished the feeling of lightness and peace before gathering the air to swing the orange chair away. I hadn't really been using much of my elemental magic until now. I used air mostly because it was the only element readily available to me. I continued to fling the different objects in various directions until I built up momentum. But Grammie stuck to her word and switched it up. The transformation of my surroundings happened in a matter of seconds; before I could blink, I was in what looked like a garbage field with many things flying around all at once. But they were all flying around at ridiculously fast speeds. I could barely concentrate on the combination of so many different sounds coming from all directions. My breath quickened and I wasn't even aware of what I was yanking or pushing away. I heard Crystiana's voice echo from wherever she was. "This is the same concept, I've just applied sounds and various objects to it."

"It is not the same!" I managed to shout back frantically. I was having to switch directions every second, trying to make sure I wasn't knocked out by an item like a fridge.

"Just use what's around you." That was all she said before going quiet once again. I groaned and furrowed my eyebrows in concentration. Use what's around you, I reminded myself. I studied my surroundings as much as I could during any moment I had between deflecting the obstacles. From what I was seeing, I had the elements of earth and air at my disposal. "Maybe…" I thought to myself as I collected dirt into a ball and used it to draw in the objects near it. I did the same thing with another set of objects and repeated until there were a dozen floating balls of soil in front of me. They were all tied together by the same dirt from the ground and held up by swirls of wind. The scene faded away and I was left panting on the floor with a film of sweat covering my forehead. I heard the sound of Crystiana clapping, and felt proud of myself. "Well done. You impressed me, I must say."

She lent me her hand to help me up and continued, "I'm glad you understood what I was trying to say. It is imperative you use what you have to the best of your abilities. For most of your life, you've been raised as a human - closed off from your real potential. But now, you have the opportunity to become something more. I suggest you make the most of that, Adira."

I blushed from seeing the pride she wore on her face because of me. "Yes, Grammie," I said.

"Good. After showering, you should eat something. I'll meet you there."

I nodded and headed off to my chambers. I paused by the door to my haven room, but realised that if I was to eat something, I wouldn't have time to meditate. So, I continued on to my chambers. It was strange, but little by little I was becoming accustomed to the place I had never thought I would get used to. There was still a lot to discover and do, but I was happy with the point I'd reached. I was proud of my progress.

I told Nora to play some music from the 1980s and for those few moments, I felt truly at home.

CHAPTER 16

GREEN

I stared at the boy with glowing green irises in the mirror. That's not me, I tried to convince myself. This is a dream. My eyes are brown. The same brown as the maple syrup I often drenched my pancakes with - at least that's what I thought. I was questioning everything at that moment, but I blacked out a second later.

Before this, everything had been normal, down to waking up to the bus driver shouting at me to get off. It had been another winter day in my town, Jinhae.

THE EARTHY FRAGRANCE of the chilly breeze greeted me as I stepped out of the bus. The petals from the nearby cherry blossom trees danced to the uncovered patches on the ground. I sauntered to the steps of the school, where my best friend, Daeun was munching on a Korean cookie. Once he saw me, he offered me a piece. I declined, knowing he'd be upset if I accepted.

We moved from class to class, our conversation revolving mostly around our plans for the Christmas holidays. It was cut short when we had to go to Biology - the only class we had without each other.

Class ended early for me, so I was waiting in the hallway for Daeun, scrolling through posts on Instagram as a distraction from my throbbing headache. Soon the words and colours meshed together, becoming distorted. I closed my eyes and opened them to see everything spinning.

I hurried to the bathroom, locking myself in a stall. I groaned as the uncomfortable feeling of needles pricking my skin attacked my entire body.

The navy blue walls surrounding me were impassive as I hugged my stomach. I squeezed my eyelids shut and saw glimpses of people fighting, green power surging through the air and creatures with gruesome appearances. When I forced them open, my veins were standing out more than ever, and I wondered if I was imagining the hints of green glowing from them.

The pain stopped as suddenly as it had started, leaving me more disoriented than ever.

I unlocked the stall and looked straight into the mirror. "Holy sh…", I managed to say, before blacking out.

A loud ringing noise woke me up. At first, everything was a

blur and the colours were indistinct. I could make out two voices at first, until the details of the people became clearer. On my right was Daeun and on my left was the nurse. I could recognise her bob of grey hair and small lips anywhere. Her face was round like Daeun's, except with more crease lines. He was talking to her, and for a short while, everything sounded garbled until I heard Daeun say, "I think he's awake."

I groaned in response, still trying to get my bearings straight. "Dude, what happened? I walked in there and you were just lying on the floor."

"I… I can't remember," I said. I frowned as I tried to see past the holes in my memory. "It was something… It was something," I muttered, "In the mirror…"

"What was in the mirror?" He asked.

I tried to remember, then panicked. "My eyes were glowing - they were glowing green."

He gave me a weird look. "Okay, now you're starting to creep me out."

"Relax…" The nurse said to Daeun, "I've seen it before. Students having nervous breakdowns due to stress often end up seeing things that aren't really there."

"I've been telling him to get more sleep. Did you know he goes to sleep at two and wakes up at…"

"I didn't have a breakdown," I interjected.

"Hush now," she said as she lightly pressed the back of her hand to my forehead.

"Your temperature is high; maybe you're coming down with a fever."

"I…"

She silenced me once again.

"It's best if you come to my office and rest up until a parent can pick you up. You shouldn't exhaust yourself too much. Here, let me help you up," she said, holding out her wrinkled hand. I took it and she pulled me up, her grip surprisingly strong for her petite figure. I looked back at Daeun, who had a look of concern on his chubby face. *What had happened while I was out?*

We arrived at her office. The sets of plush furniture made it homey. There were lots of windows; most were open and rays of sunshine poured into the room through the open blinds. I heard the door lock behind me and turned to see her stubby features morph from a round, porcelain face, framed with grey hair to a dark-haired, female with slanted eyes. She didn't give me a chance to react and wasted no time before blowing gold dust in my face. It clouded my vision and soon all I saw was blackness.

When I had seen Daeun's scared face in reaction to my episode, I didn't realise it would be the last time I'd see him. Although, if he had reacted like that back then, he would probably faint if he had any idea of the world I was in now.

CHAPTER 17

PINK

I headed to the dimly lit chambers with grand pillars and colossal shelves stacked with books. There I found Crystiana buried in books as usual. This time she was simultaneously rearranging them with her magic and reading one.

"Grammie?" I asked, even though it was likely she had sensed me when I'd entered.

My voice jolted her out of whatever trance she was in and she said, "Hello dear, have a seat."

Once I'd taken a seat on the hovering, cushioned platform, she sat opposite me and activated the hologram system.

On this day, we went through the deeper history of the Triphants and the major conflicts of the universe. She mentioned that it was essential I learned this so that I knew the basic principles of which species to befriend and which ones I shouldn't. I felt more confident after the lesson; I felt it had led me one step closer to finding my place in this world. Clorista had quickly grown to be my home.

After meditating for some time in my haven, I drifted off and found myself somewhere that wasn't my safe place. It was a vision, something that had become rare in my time at Clorista.

I was drifting through a dimly lit cavern in which hovering creatures wearing black cloaks were stationed in corners.

I drifted over to the centre, where there was a glowing being sitting on a black and gold throne which had sculptures of red snakes swirling around it. I squinted to see past the strong glow of its magic and saw an ethereal creature with pointed ears and red scales printed on its forehead. It had long, flowing scarlet hair with blonde highlights. Its eyes were feminine and its nose was sharp and straight. I was beginning to recognise it as a female.

She was sitting in an elegant and graceful manner. She looked like a queen and I supposed I was right, judging by the fact that she was on a throne. When I got closer, I felt immense waves of magic rolling off of her. I was able to make out the little details at this point.

She wore a thin, flowing black dress that split along her thighs. She was looking at someone or something. Her eyes were gold and red freckles were scattered all over her golden face. I drifted almost in front of her and turned to see who she was staring at. It was the same honey-coloured hair and blue eyes that had once pierced my soul.

"Jake," I whispered. I could almost swear I saw his jaw clench, but he remained passive. He looked as if he had been drained and his usually-plump skin resembled ash. He'd lost a significant amount of weight. I heard a scratchy voice come from behind me; it reeked of dark

magic. "Raeden, all of this is for you. It's incompetent of you not to have noticed that yet." When she addressed him with that name, I could see his eye twitch ever so slightly.

"Yes, but what if I don't want this?" he asked.

"You don't want all the power and control you could ever have?" She scoffed, "You are no son of mine if you think that way."

His head lowered and he mumbled, "According to the triphant law-"

"I'm your mother!" she scolded, "Are you really going to listen to those creatures over me? Only I know what's best for you."

I frowned. This being was not a triphant, she was something else entirely, but the strangest thing was the faint triphant aura I sensed from her.

"But I can't ignore the triphant law or..."

"They took you from me, remember?"

"Yes, but-"

"But, what?" Her eyes narrowed.

"The penalty is death. If I do this, then I'll be hunted down by guardians."

"Nonsense." She brushed it off with the gesture of her hand and continued, "You should know that if they were to even breathe on you, they would be obliterated in seconds."

"Yes, mother."

She turned her intense gaze away from Jake and instructed, "Again."

At first, he struggled to create a spark of his magic, but when it finally came to him, it flowed fluid and strong.

My focus shifted to the large stone that glowed when he used his magic. It possessed his energy and it was blue - the same blue as his beautiful, sunken eyes.

"Just know, Raeden, it's taken me years to get where I am now. I don't plan to let that all go to waste."

The scene faded as she made that bitter statement.

My eyelids fluttered open. During the time I had been out, a film of cold sweat had covered my forehead.

What could his mother want him to do that would make guardians have to kill him?

Was Jake trying to communicate with me?

It could be my mind making up stuff, but in this world, I had learned that nothing was a coincidence. If that was really happening to him, why hadn't he reached out to me sooner?

Questions: there were so many questions racing through my head. I hurried out of my haven, which wasn't feeling so therapeutic anymore and into my other space, where I could talk to Nora and have her play some music, which would fill my head with other things besides my thoughts.

When I reached my chambers, I peeled off the training suit and hopped into the shower. I couldn't be bothered with a bath.

Once I slipped on some light blue pyjamas, an intense misery came over me. I couldn't help but feel the growing, aching hole in my heart. There were surges of disappointment every time I reminded myself that it was one-sided. He hadn't seen me in the vision or whatever it was. "Scene to the Atlas Mountains, please," I mumbled to Nora.

It was the last place Jake and I had been together: during the few, cherished moments I'd spent leaning against him, feeling his precious warmth and smelling his sweet scent of cinnamon and vanilla. I sat down in front of the broad windows and admired the view. Though the scene lacked the cool breeze and smell of fresh grass, the scattered dots of light sparkling in the night sky displayed on my ceiling made up for it.

Soon, my eyes turned into kaleidoscopes and the tears began t fall, one by one. They were silent tears, full of pain and frustration. When it became too painful to remember him, I instructed Nora to turn it off and climbed into my soft, warm bed.

I sighed as I lay in the darkness of my chambers, alone and wistful as ever. I took a deep breath and closed my eyes to take a break from staring at the aurora lights being displayed on the ceiling. I thought about the many experiences I'd had over the past few months, ever since Jake took me from Rosie, my mum's best friend, and into the triphant world. I thought about the people I'd lost and the friendships I'd sacrificed to get to where I was now. No matter how painful it was, this reminder gave me the drive and strength I needed to keep going. I had to do it; the immense amount of effort I was putting into training had to be worth something.

I succumbed to the darkness and fell into a deep sleep.

When my eyes flickered open, I expected to see my chambers. Instead, I saw stalls squished alongside each other and many signs of foreign writing. The place was full of chatter and unfamiliar accents. There was an abundance of cherry blossom petals on the many trees that surrounded the area. I knew I wasn't actually there as, when I came in front of a stall, the old lady stationed by it continued to shove her crispy, fried fish sticks into people's faces. I tried picking one up and my hand passed through the table as if it wasn't even there. When I saw her take some more out of her frying pan, I expected to smell the delightful aroma of the chicken, but nothing came. I couldn't smell anything but I still heard and saw everything. After a short while, I realized they couldn't see me.

I frowned, wondering what I was doing there when I heard a whisper urging me to follow. I thought twice before following it.

"Adira..." it said, "Come here..."

I headed in the direction of the voice; as I got closer, it grew quieter. After passing the many stalls of various spices, steaming food, candy and merchandise, I left the market. In the path I was on, the cherry blossom trees hid most of the cloudless, cerulean blue sky above and I could only imagine their sweet scent. Their petals were blanketing the ground. I was heading to what looked like the entrance to a tunnel; as I approached it, the whispers stopped.

I headed back down to the path to see what would happen and the whispers began once again. It was the tunnel that was calling me, I was sure of it now. If I was there in real life, I probably wouldn't have entered, but in the subconscious realm, I felt it was okay to be careless.

The dank tunnel was as dark as I expected it to be and, as I went deeper inside, the light streaming in from outside began to fade until I was left in nothing but darkness. In the subconscious realm, I realised my body had an ethereal glow that lit up a small radius around me. In the faint light I was emitting, I could see black coal scattered on the ground. As I drifted through the tunnel, I tried to imagine the crunching sound.

As I was heading further into the cave, I noticed footprints in the ground. Who else was here? *It seemed as if the gods had heard my question; soon I could see a faint green light in the distance. It only took me a few seconds to realise what this was all about, why I had randomly appeared in this place. The random voice wanted to show me where Green was. I gasped as he looked up to me with his glowing green irises.*

I woke up with a gasp, a film of cold sweat coating my forehead as greeting me as usual.

I had to tell Crystiana immediately.

CHAPTER 18

GREEN

All I could see was a purple light and a lady staring at me. The same lady who had taken me away from my hometown.

"Who are you? Where are we?" I asked. I was panicking. Too many things were happening at once.

She placed a cold hand on my back and said, "Sit up."

I shrugged her hand off brusquely and got up. "Don't ever touch me again," I said.

She didn't even flinch. Instead, her expression remained passive and I felt a sudden urge to cry. Seeing her with such a lack of care frustrated me.

"Where are we?" I asked, my voice cracking in the middle of the question.

"In the waiting realm," she answered calmly as if she hadn't just taken me away from my life.

I looked around. My heart seemed to be beating outside of my chest.

"What the hell is the waiting realm?" I felt like screaming, shouting, anything to get away from here.

"HELP!" I screamed.

"HELP!" I screamed again. I kept yelling until I realised no one was coming to get me. I looked at her, my heart weighing heavier than ever.

She hadn't even bothered to stop me.

She knew no one was coming - that they would never come because there was no one here to begin with. "Please," I begged. The warm tears broke through my weak barrier and crept down my face.

It was only then that she frowned and said, "You shouldn't cry, Green. You should be honoured."

"Who the hell is Green?" My eyes widened. "You have the wrong person," I blurted out, "It's not me. Please, take me back. Please."

"You have been chosen by the Green universal stone. You are one of the chosen. A half-breed, but a member of the chosen nonetheless."

My eyebrows knitted together. "I don't understand. Is this some sort of experiment or are you just sick in the head?"

"I assure you it is not and I am perfectly well. I am a watcher and, as you were chosen, I have been assigned to look after you until you are in Crystiana's possession."

"A watcher?"

"It is a triphant job. One that requires great understanding. I take great pride in it, as you should in yours."

"A triphant job?" This lady was spewing more nonsense by the second. I could almost feel my brain cells decreasing the more she talked.

"It is a job of a race hidden away from human knowledge, gifted with supernatural abilities, including time travel, by the time gods."

Ha.

"And who's Crystiana?" I questioned.

"The one who will train you to become the greatest Green to ever have existed."

There it was again. "My name is Kyung-Dae… and you still sound sick."

"Then there is no point in conversing with you anymore, Green. Either way, if it is your friends or family on Earth that you wish to see, then just know you have been erased from their memories. No one on Earth knows who you are, not anymore."

My heart skipped a beat. "No, you're lying," I gulped, "I'm not believing it until I see it."

"Are you sure of your request? I know all about young human emotions."

"What?"

She sighed and said, "Come with me."

She began to walk off and I had no choice but to follow her. As much as I disliked her, she was my only ticket out of there.

I recognised this place as my hometown, yet it seemed so

alien to me. Everything was stagnant, not to mention the otherworldly glow that was far from Earth's appearance.

"Where are you taking me?" I asked.

"I'm showing you what you asked to see," she quipped.

A bright light shone in front of me and I blocked it with my forearm. When the light had ceased, I looked around again.

We were no longer in the waiting realm but in my kitchen. "You took me back?"

My face broke into a smile and suddenly her dark eyes no longer looked heartless but loving. Her face no longer looked hollow and sharp but strong and feminine. Her hair no longer looked limp, but shiny and full in her sleek, high ponytail. Her jewellery no longer seemed threatening, but rather attractive in the way it gleamed in the sunlight. She opened her bronze-coated mouth to say something, but my mother entered.

"Ma, I'm home. I did not feel well today. So, she took me home," I started and gestured to the lady.

She didn't acknowledge me, despite me being a few metres away at best.

"Ma, I know I haven't been as helpful around the house as you've wanted me to be, but I promise you that stops today."

Normally, she would have looked at me and smiled with creases on the sides of her honey-brown eyes. Instead, she finished putting the dishes into the cupboard and walked straight past me.

Shivers raced down my spine.

When I followed her out of the room, I realised she hadn't just passed me; she'd walked straight through me.

It was as if I didn't exist…

"No, you can't be right. This can't be happening," I gulped, "Ma?"

She continued to ignore me as she tugged on her tiny, plaid-patterned shoes that hugged her stubby feet. They were the same feet she would ask me to massage for her after a long day at work.

My heart raced and the panic rose and squeezed my throat. It rose and blurred my vision when I looked at the wall behind her. The wall was supposed to have a framed photo of the two of us sitting with Santa. It was gone.

It was bare.

I hadn't seen it that bare since my seven-year-old self had helped put it up with her. I remembered the Christmas music playing softly in the background. I looked back at her; she was just grabbing her keys. There were only her shoes, mine were not there. But maybe she had just rearranged the house. I grabbed her wrist as she turned the key. I couldn't let her leave.

"Ma, I'm right here." My hand passed straight through as if I was grabbing air. My breaths quickened and my throat grew tighter. I hurried up the steps and into my room.

My "room" was now an office. It was filled to the brim with books and boxes. "No," I muttered again.

I felt her presence a few metres behind me. I wasn't sure how, but I sensed her power as if it was a pinprick on my skin.

"What did you do?" I asked, my voice cracked in the middle of it.

"I didn't do anything. This is a result of the time gods."

I opened my mouth to say something, but no words came out. I was scared if I moved too much, the tears would flow and never stop. I refused to believe it was real.

"I would like to leave." I finally managed to say.

"As you wish."

She snapped her fingers and brought us to somewhere else entirely, but in that moment I was thankful to be anywhere but there. It was simply too painful.

CHAPTER 19

PINK

It was the fastest I'd ever gotten dressed in all of my time at Clorista and my sense of peace was gone as it had now been replaced with a sense of urgency.

I had found him and now it was my job to get him to Clorista.

Crystiana met my frantic state with her usual calm and collected demeanour. "Yes, Adira," she said, "What is it you would like to tell me?"

"I found him," I said.

"Jake?"

Hearing her say his name brought the pain back, and I couldn't help but feel disappointed as I said, "No, Green."

Her pleasant facial expression tightened into a grim one. With the snap of her fingers, she teleported us to the library.

"How?"

"It was some sort of vision, I'm not sure exactly, but I know it was him. He had the same aura and his irises glowed green, just like mine glow pink and Red's glow red."

"I also received something from a watcher. That was him. Describe the message, from the top."

I paused as I noted the way she called it a message instead of a vision. "OK... Well, it started in a marketplace..." I started, and as I spoke, she activated the hologram system to form an image of what I was explaining. "There were petals from the cherry blossom trees scattered in heaps. There were stalls selling things like spices, candy and fried chicken. The language they spoke wasn't English, it was something different..."

Crystiana nodded as if she knew what I was talking about. "Did the language look like this?" She asked as she switched the progressive image to one that had symbols on it. I nodded. "It seems you're describing a place in South Korea; continue."

"Afterwards, I heard whispers telling me to follow, so I did. I ventured out of the market, and soon I was on a path, where the cherry blossom trees covered the sky. Then, I reached a tunnel. It was really dark and my sight was limited. I could only see coal and some footprints as well. That's when I saw the faint green light and then I saw him."

When I was done explaining, the hologram had designed a strangely accurate image that depicted the exact place I had travelled to.

"Now that we've found him, it seems I must move on to the next phase of your training."

"What's that?"

"Portal jumping. I was going to introduce you to it soon, but now it is clear I must prioritise it."

"Jake once did a portal jump. I hated it," I admitted.

She chuckled, "It's a bit unpleasant at first, I must say, but once you get the hang of it, it can be quite the experience. Anyway, we need about three days to get you sharp enough to portal jump and retrieve him. We've worked a lot on your control, discipline and reflexes, so it shouldn't be too hard for you to grasp the concept."

I nodded.

"I'll have Nora wake you up earlier tomorrow. We have to go through many things. For now, let's start from the basics of portal jumping."

She teleported us to the training chambers and for a while, I had to do various drills repeatedly until she let me take a break and try something else altogether. "Now that you're sharp and warmed up, we'll start." She waved her hand and muttered something inaudible; when she finished chanting, my gemstone appeared in her palm. "Here you are, dear."

"Whoa…" I mumbled as the warmth of my gemstone seeped into me. After all this time, I finally realised what the warmth was. It was the gemstone's magic flowing into me. It was a comforting type of warmth and it made me feel safe. It was like an exhilarating rush; after the warmth came the adrenaline and sharpness in my senses. The thrill felt almost like an ongoing joy ride.

"Thank you."

"It was time you got it back; also, with the amount of magic you'll be using, you'll need to keep it on you so can keep going."

Just as she mentioned magic, I gathered a swirling ball of energy in my palm and watched as it grew. It was one thing to make an electricity ball, but it was another to sustain it. Sustaining one was the human equivalent of holding one's breath, and I could only hold it for 30 seconds before getting dizzy. Now with my gemstone, I had been able to hold it for one minute and counting.

"Impressive, but you shouldn't waste your energy on that. I can tell you're eager to use your magic, but all in due course," she said.

She brought up an image of people opening portals twice the size of them and continued, "Portal jumping was a concept created near the beginning to get from one area on a planet to another. To do this, you needed the image of where they were going and the power to get you there. A normal triphant would need to team up with a couple of others to do so, but as a chosen one, your power source might as well be limitless. However, there is only so much one can take; that is why even the chosen have to take breaks. To become good at portal jumping, there is one thing you *must* do."

"What's that?"

"Practice. If you do not practice a skill once you learn it, you will soon find it hard to recall how to do it at all. Portal jumping becomes increasingly risky the further you go as there are more places in between. Fortunately, Clorista has no in-between realms or space gaps, so you'll be fine. But when going down to

Earth, if you lose focus during the jump, the consequences could be catastrophic."

As she finished that statement, her facial expression tightened as if she had witnessed it before.

"Grammie, I have a question."

"Go ahead, dear,"

"If any triphant can portal jump, what makes Red's ability so special?"

"Ah… Good question. You see, triphants can only portal jump to places they've been before, and only to planets. Red can portal to realms, space gaps and the places in between; she can travel somewhere only having seen it once. It also doesn't matter if Red has been to the place or not as her gemstone has been to many places in its lifetime, sharing the memories of all the other Reds."

"So, you're saying that if I wanted to, I could…"

"See your mother's memories?"

"Yeah…"

"Yes, but only once you've reached the peak of your magic, when your gemstone's magic will finish connecting with you and you and it will become one with you."

"When would that happen?"

"It could happen on any of your birthdays from now on," she said.

"OK." She continued to guide me through the basics of portal jumping; for a while it was just me practising visualising things, and learning to use my memory to my advantage.

After this, she told me to portal jump to my bedroom. As I

had visualised my bedroom for what seemed like a hundred times, I never expected the cold sweat to be forming on my forehead or the feeling that I was going to puke. No matter how much I tried to create the portal, it put an uncomfortable strain on me and I found myself panting after only a few seconds of sustaining the sparkling circle of magic.

"When was the last time you ate, Adira?" Grammie asked.

It had me frowning as I tried to remember. "I'm not sure," I admitted.

She raised her eyebrow disapprovingly and snapped her fingers. She had teleported us to the dining chambers, "Eat something." I sighed and followed her instructions. I went through the first course faster than I ever had. I drank every remaining bit of the chicken soup and licked my fingers from the spicy, fried lobster. I had eaten enough to be able to slow down and have a conversation with Grammie while eating.

"The teleporting thing you do," I started while chomping into a wrap. "The one when you snap your fingers and we arrive in different places."

"Mhm." She replied while taking her time to finish her chicken soup.

"Why can't you just... teleport me to Green?"

She seemed to be perturbed by the question I asked. "Because..." She paused and I watched as she patted her mouth with a handkerchief. "What would happen if you were alone and you didn't have someone to help you portal? What would you do then?"

"Yes, but I was just wondering if you could teleport me and then after…"

"No. It is crucial for you to learn by yourself before I ever offer to do something for you."

I was thrown off by her tone; suddenly I'd lost my appetite, despite the crunchiness of the juicy salamar in my wrap. It resembled salami on Earth, except with a distinct flavor.

"I understand."

We ate in silence and she left me to practise my visualisation exercises until she came back.

The visualisation exercises were exhausting and I found myself taking frequent breaks from the strain it was putting on my mind. I understood I had to push myself, but the mental training was more brutal than I could have imagined. I wasn't sure if I could keep it up for much longer; it worried me as she had said to keep going until she came back.

As I did the exercises more and more, I yearned for my magic to keep me going, but soon my eyelids grew heavy and I knew I had worn myself out for the day. I hoped for my birthday to come soon, so I had at least a chance at coming out of this shell and fully bonding with my gemstone. I stumbled to my bedroom, ignoring my haven for today and, after stripping off my training suit, I climbed into bed and blacked out.

My heart raced as I heard a voice in my head telling me it was time to wake up. It took me a while to figure out it was Nora and I calmed down. Just as Grammie had said, Nora had woken me up earlier than usual.

I had a pounding headache. Headaches were no longer a bother to me as they would go away once I drank some crystal water. It was everywhere in Clorista and all I needed to do was turn on my tap. I gulped a mouthful and caught a glimpse of myself in the mirror. I hadn't noticed it, but little by little, the glow of my skin had become more apparent. It was almost as if I was an angel. I smiled at myself, turning from side to side and looking in the mirror while my headache ebbed away. I knew that there was no time to waste and soon I was rushing out of my chambers to the training chambers, where Grammie had a simulation that looked like an abundant source of orange dots set up.

"Welcome Adira," she said, "I think this activity will help develop your magic-eye coordination."

As soon as I stepped onto the polished wooden floor, I entered another world. It was bright and eerie. I could hear birds chirping and see the leaves glistening in the light. Though everything seemed real, I could still smell Clorista's subtle sweet scent.

"Today you'll be playing a memory game. You'll be using teleportation, which requires less magic than a portal jump, so it will be easier to become second nature to you. Allow me to explain how this works," she moved the scene to another place with a river and looming white trees and continued, "In this game, you will have 30 minutes to memorise everything in the place you arrive in. Knowing what everything looks like, it should be easy enough for you to teleport there. Each round, the place gets bigger and there are more things for you to memorise, let's see how far you can get on your first time." She gave me a wry smile and disappeared, leaving me alone in the simulation.

"I have 30 minutes," I whispered and used what Jake had taught me to set an internal timer. I gently pressed on my wrist with two fingers and four zeros appeared. I set it to "*30 00*" by pressing on it a few times and started wandering around.

CHAPTER 20

RED

*S*aph had opened the ceiling and the mellowy light from the stars shone down onto the current book I was reading. Over the past few days, I had successfully read the entire library's worth of books on the demon realm- hundreds of stories consisting of different types of nothing.

Yes, I had learned of some more species residing in the demon realm and two abilities of the demon king- glamour and mind control. But, I was yet to come across anything about Reina and what she was up to.

My current read was a journal written by a Past Red. Saph said it had randomly appeared. I highly suspected it was courtesy of Madella. So, of course, I couldn't help myself from seeing what it was about. I was right in the middle when Saph announced something about finding another new book. She placed it gently beside me and I muttered something in response, too engrossed in what I was reading to really pay attention.

So far, Red had defeated the alpha dragon and was heading out of Argon to attend a meeting being hosted in the triphant realm. It was a very rare time when all of the chosen ones met, but she was told it was a dire matter that involved the universe's fate.

According to what she'd been told, Yellow was hosting it in the Africa gateway and she had portalled there at the same time as Green. She'd never met Yellow before but had previously worked on the same mission as Green- closing up wormholes in the Aen galaxy. She and Green were on good terms so when she saw the sharp cheekbones, long, wavy grey hair invaded with streaks of brown, she made sure to hug the slim figure.

I was reading faster now, skimming over some of the details as I had already been to the Africa gateway. The most important thing as of right now was finding out why the meeting was so important, requiring Yellow to retrieve the chosen ones from places halfway across the galaxy.

They were in a dark room and Yellow's ebony skin was hard to make out. She said the tension was so thick it could be sliced with a knife.

Flick.

Flick.

More nonsense.

Flick.

Wait. I flicked back to the page before where I caught the word 'prophecy'.

. . .

"The book- it glowed today", he said.

"Show us the new prophecy," she said.

When he opened the book, it flicked to a page with cursive writing that glowed amber.

"I didn't want to open it until we were all here, in case it jinxed anything," he said.

Normally I would have laughed, knowing what polar opposites we were.

He was superstitious while I believed more in fate.

If something was meant to happen, it was going to happen.

We all read the miniature handwriting and when I read the word 'war', I gasped, along with Green. Yellow's eyebrows simply knitted together. The prophecy stated that the rebirth of a hybrid would declare the beginning of a war between balance and chaos.

"A hybrid…" Green started, her raspy voice interrupting the uncomfortable silence. "What does this mean?"

"It means war is coming," Yellow replied.

"But for this to happen… an abomination of nature would have to be created," I concluded.

I stopped reading at that point because it was right there that everything clicked.

Jake was a hybrid. No, he was *the* hybrid. Reina created a hybrid on the side of chaos.

She wanted to rebirth Jake.

I got a flashback to the blue baby I had to retrieve from the demon realm all those years ago.

Was it possible that that was him?

If she had already rebirthed him, the war had already begun. It was just a matter of time before they arrived. It was obvious now that there was no more time to waste. Everything from now on had to be a part of a calculated plan if we wanted to defeat this greater evil. The time had come for me to use my powers for the greater good with no room for mistakes.

"I found it," I announced whilst wearing a grim expression.

"Found what?" Saph asked. She looked puzzled.

"I haven't found a way to defeat her, but I know of her weakness and strength. Crazy enough, I met him. He left me though. If I had known he had left to go to Reina…" I groaned and met her purple eyes. "I need to get him back. The fate of the universe depends on it."

"I understand. So what does this mean? You're leaving?"

"I have to. It's clear my time in this palace is up. Madella will simply have to understand."

I got up and packed the books and scribbles I wrote on the papers into two piles. "Thank you for your help, Saph. You have no idea how much you've done."

Tears welled up in her eyes and I turned around to leave. "I'm coming with you," she blurted.

"Don't be ridiculous." I turned to face her and continued, "You're not even halfway ready to think about war, much less join it. Besides, I think that's a conversation meant for your mother."

"Wait," I heard her soft voice say.

"Mhm?"

"There's something I think you should know about my father."

My face grew grim. "Tell me."

She explained his nightly trips out and how he disappeared each night without a trace. He mumbled dark spells under his breath and how his aura grew darker each day that passed.

"Thank you for telling me," I said after she'd finished explaining the situation.

"Please don't leave me here."

I wiped the blue tear that fell from her eye and said, "Don't cry. You'll be fine, I promise."

"I'll be lonely," she whispered and I sensed her anger.

"I'll come back for you."

"Promise?"

"I promise." If not for Saphella, then for the fire pixies.

I left the library and hurried down the steps. "Madella!" I called. "Made-"

"Yes," she interjected.

I turned around to face her and said, "It's time I leave. I'll be needing access to my gemstone now."

She was wearing a sheer lilac dress that clung to her curves and her wavy black hair fell to her hips. "Why would I give that back to you?"

I paused to glare into her pale purple eyes and take in her sharp features, before saying, "I knew you wouldn't do it, which is why I had to learn to do it myself." I snapped my fingers and broke the magical barrier around the gemstone. I felt the warmth of its magic seep into my body. "I missed that."

"How did you know?"

"I found it in the spellbook you gave me. You forgot to cover it up."

"So you did read through all of it."

"Why wouldn't I?"

She sighed. "I must say your presence has been refreshing. It's sad to see you go." She made a gesture with her hand and a door swung open, revealing a shadowed alleyway to the Autumn court. I'd adapted to the dim lighting so the bright light of the outside world blinded me for a couple of seconds. I shielded the shocking, vivid colours with my hand. "One last thing though," I said before stepping through the door. "Whatever you do, do not trust Razel. I have a very strong feeling he is working with Reina- that he has been since the day she visited. Look at the west wing footage for proof. You should assume he knows everything and if he does, she does. The war has begun. Figure out what you're doing and fast."

When I stepped out of the door, I looked back at her distraught expression and added, "Thank you for your time."

The door swung shut before me and I grabbed my black concealing cloak from the athen box, swiftly slipping it on.

I joined the crowd in the middle part of the court where there were the most people. I weaved through the crowd of people and avoided the many little tornados being conjured and miniature faeries. I got a few stares every now and then, but maybe it was because of my fast pace. Everyone in this part was rushing, but not like I was.

Floating lanterns were being held in the air by little swirls of wind, emitting golden light in their small proximity. The night was approaching fast and preparations were being made for a party. I glanced up to see a full pink moon, a reason to celebrate according to the faeries. Moondust shimmered on their bodies, reflecting in the lights around us. Their mirth was palpable as they danced to the music being played on wind instruments.

Whistles were sent swirling through the air as I passed. Some were distinct while others were faint.

I had no idea when the demons would start attacking so my top priority was getting the news to Lord Theo as soon as possible. My fast pace became even more noticeable when I had entered the wealthy part of the court.

The sounds were muted and there was little activity except for the occasional laugh. Most of the rich faeries spent their time in the palaces they built for themselves, only coming out for the frequent exclusive parties. Instead of paying mind to the scrutinizing stares, I was busy thinking of how I was going to start such a crucial message and not make it sound ridiculous. I needed him to take me seriously.

When I neared the castle, it was almost as if the temperature dropped and everything became dull and grey. I slowed when I stood in front of the looming, uninviting black gates that towered a couple of feet over me with a line of manicured rose bushes complimenting them. A shrunken faerie flew over the gate and appeared full-size in front of me.

"Who are you and what brings you here?" They questioned.

This faerie had braided auburn locs that stretched down to their waist. They wore the typical autumn uniform that consisted of a green tunic, dark brown loose pants and a sheer, olive green scarf wrapped around their neck. Their sculpted face had an inner glow, complimenting their moss-green eyes. I wasn't going to assume the gender as the beauty standards were different in the faerie world, thus making the genders look more similar than ever. I switched to the faerie language and said, "I'm here to see the faerie lord."

They scoffed. "So you're not only bold but you're an idiot."

"Excuse me?"

"You dare step foot on holy ground with the desire to *see* the faerie lord. Only the higher ranks have the privilege to stroll in here daily. I demand you leave here at once, you have wasted my time."

I realised my mistake as soon as they said it. I was still concealing my magic with the cloak. As far as they were concerned I was an outsider with no magic, those were considered even less than a peasant. I was surprised they had even responded to me. I peeled off the cloak and their eyes widened.

My scarlet red tank top and glossy black jacket were now exposed, along with my black pants and pair of boots.

"It's you."

My eyes glowed scarlet red when I conjured a portal ball in my hand. "Either you let me in, or I go in myself and I'm sure you don't want a gaping hole in your gate," I said.

"Open the gates," they shouted. The doors opened inwards shortly after and I strolled in- the small, cream-coloured stones crunching under my feet.

A chilly breeze blew through my clothes and my gemstone regulated my body temperature so I was no colder or no hotter than when I entered. Rose bushes lined both sides of the broad path. Beyond that, were fields of unruly viridescent grass wearing a blanket of leaves ranging from a lush green to mauve purple. A large number of trees dotted the landscape and gave the sun a fight to shine through their leaves.

The sweet, musky scent of the roses wafted into my nostrils. They were the Lord's favourite flowers and they were scattered everywhere in his court. The faerie flew alongside me in their minimised size, their translucent wings tinted blue. "I know it's not my business, but what is so important that one of the chosen must come to the faerie realm?"

Their meek demeanour suggested they already knew the answer. They probably wanted confirmation.

"War."

They went silent and the tension between us only grew from there. "I see," they said after a while. We reached the mahogany brown marble steps and the towering grey doors opened to reveal a grand entryway. "My name is Anthea," she blurted after a short while. She had grown to her full size again and towered over me by a few inches.

"It's a pleasure to meet you," I replied. Once I recognised the femininity in their name, I instantly noticed her slender collarbones and slight curves.

As soon as we stepped onto the plush red rug the doors shut softly behind us. I no longer felt the breeze on my skin, but the cosy temperature of the palace. The pathways were dimly lit by torches on the side of each black wall. They slightly illuminated the family portraits lining the walls.

It took a while of walking for us to reach any doors. After passing many chambers, we arrived at a colossal-sized stone door with a split down its middle.

I assumed it was the entry to the Lord's throne room. "Wait here," she whispered. She shrunk down into her miniature size and passed through the small gap in the middle.

I took the time to pay attention to the area around me. In this part of the palace, the path extended to a greenhouse. I could see plants moving beyond the tinted, thick glass and tried to figure out which plant was which from the spot I was in.

There was more light here. A huge chandelier hung from the low ceiling. It showed the rug was actually a rich tone of burgundy, lined with gold. The patterns on the black walls weren't just swirls but drawings of faeries interacting with each other.

There was a faint sound of the faeries talking and music being played, beyond the walls. After a while of waiting in the dimly lit corridor, the doors blasted open and I was introduced to a large hall flooded with light from the clear windows. The floral scent of roses slammed into my face stronger than ever as I saw various species of rose bushes hanging from the ceiling. Their petals decorated the floor with patches of colours ranging from lilac to mustard yellow.

Lord Theo lay slouched in his red throne decorated with gold. When I entered, it was like I didn't even exist, the way continued laughing and joking around with his right hand in command. His joyful laughter was the only sound that could be heard besides the music being played on flutes and the occasional mutter from his second-in-hand, which looked awfully frail. He held a silver goblet in his left hand and plopped red cherries into his mouth with the other. There were a number of female faeries braiding each other's hair with some kind of blue jelly-like substance. Lord Theo seemed to be swatting away Anteah as if she were a pest. Maybe she was trying to tell him I was here, not that he didn't sense me from a mile away. I continued forward, my steps silenced by the carpet of petals. Once I'd neared a few metered within his presence, his laughter died down immediately and he waved everyone out. The melodic tunes being played by the flutes stopped abruptly and his face grew solemn. "What do you want?" He asked. It was as if my very presence had irritated him and maybe it did, but I could care less. "I am here to warn you. A prophecy was stated by Present; a hybrid has been born and the war between balance and chaos has begun. I will need allies on the side of balance."

"Well, duh. Do I even have a choice in the matter?"

I stayed silent. I was in a realm filled with master manipulators, anything I said could be used against me.

He sighed. "Whatever. I'll gather my army and warn my people."

"Good. For now, stay alert. They could attack at any given time. They could already be here."

I turned on my heel and headed out. "Tell Crystiana I said hi."

"Sure," I muttered and opened a portal to Runningbird. I was hoping Lord Huricus would be as accepting as Lord Theo. Runningbird was significantly more modern and was under stricter control. It was very unlike the Autumn Court which seemed to have parties every other day. I could feel the thick tension in the air when I entered. One could say Lord Huricus had a totalitarian rule over his court. I didn't bother putting the cloak back on. I was done hiding. It was time to make a statement.

And I did.

Faeries stopped to stare. The moderate chatter died down in an instant and I felt their gazes follow my every step. The crowd split to give me a clear path, down to the young faeries. They all knew who I was. They had felt my magic every day of their lives, surrounding their realm. I reached the shiny, navy blue gates and this time the faeries at the sides opened them immediately. After reading the previous Red's journal, I knew that respect was not given out easily, but fought for. Lord Huricus was extra with his display. Within a few metres of smooth, fawn ground, there was a series of steps made up of air that led up to his palace. His palace cast a huge shadow onto the slate ground underneath. I hopped onto the steps one by one and the thick, silver doors opened inwards. For someone who was strict with the lifestyles of the people, he seemed very comfortable with his security. I strolled in and there was a chilly draft blowing through the halls.

Whispers surrounded me and chanted,

"Follow the red fly".

A red fly materialised in front of me and just like the whispers said, I followed it. It went against every fibre of my being but I did so anyway. I supposed it was a safety precaution of the faerie lord. It led me through the many grey corridors. Until I swore it was leading me around in circles. My blood began to boil with anger.

"You think I'm a fool?" I asked, projecting my voice so there was a good chance of him hearing me. It was likely that he was nearby. I heard a loud and jarring laugh bounce off of the silver walls.

"Ah, Red. Let me have my fun, will you?" He said, the cockiness in his tone was unmistakably Lord Huricus.

"I am not here to entertain your childish tricks."

"Then to what do I owe the pleasure?" He asked.

"War is coming." I wasn't sure where he was and I'd been talking to a plain wall in front of me. A door beside me appeared and opened, revealing a grand lounge, chilled by a draught. He materialised in front of me, greeting me with a gust of wind.

"I'm listening," I replied.

"Some time ago, Present prophesied that the time would come when balance and chaos would fight to determine the fate of the universe. This fight will take place on the home planet, Earth. Choose balance and fight with me. It is imperative we win, or life as you know it will cease to exist."

His eyebrows dug into his forehead. "Why now? Out of all the decades... out of all the centuries, why now?" He asked.

"A hybrid has been born, linking the chaos realm to the motherland, that was the start of the prophecy."

"I see. Well... I'll gather my troops."

"Good, stay on guard. It won't be long before they find a way to infiltrate the faerie realm."

"And what's stopping you from strengthening the barrier?"

"Ah... See, I need to conserve my magic, and that takes the strength of not just me, but another chosen triphant altogether. Also, if I strengthen the barrier, and they get in, I'll have a harder time bringing it down to free the fae. Long story short, they're bound to find a way in and when that happens, I'm sure you won't want to stick around."

"Well, we've all heard the story of the Founding War and I'm sure it won't be a stroll in the park like it was back then. This time, a lot more is at risk and I want something in return."

"Before you dare to ask for something in return, I suggest you worry about what the chaos will do to your people." I had had enough and formed a portal to the right side of us.

His lips formed a thin line and he clenched his jaw. "*If* I survive, I would like my people and me to be free. This is a cage, Red. I don't know how much longer I can take it."

"Oh, you'll be free alright, so don't worry about that. If you excuse me, I have to talk to the others. Hopefully, they won't waste my time as you did."

I dismissed him and I stepped into the portal and into Bellbon.

CHAPTER 21

PINK

I had arrived on a straight dirt path that stretched into the foggy distance.

I was taking mental notes of everything, down to the mahogany bark scattered throughout the dark brown dirt. There was a forest on my left and a field on my right. I supposed there would be specific objects that would disappear, so I paid keen attention to where certain trees were placed.

I noticed there were only seven trees placed in a zigzag pattern next to each other. I made sure to tear off bark from the trunk in specific places so I could identify them when the moment came. Once I was done with the forest, I faced the field of wheat and tall grass. I looked at the time I had left on my wrist; it read, "*21 29*".

I was making good time, but I knew the field could very well be a maze. So, I hurried into the swaying, tall grass. It covered most of my view of the murky sky. I let prickling sensations all over as I rushed through it. It felt like I had been hurrying through it for aeons; when I checked my clock, it read "*18 34*", I sighed in relief and continued at the same pace so I wouldn't tire myself out.

The ground grew increasingly muddy; it was getting harder to lift my feet, so my pace slowed significantly. There were a few rocks. I had tried my best to avoid them, but eventually I tripped over one and stumbled into what looked like the centre of the field.

There was no tall grass in the circle of dirt. Instead, there were items placed far away from each other. I hopped over to one that was white and glowing and saw it was a snowman. I frowned as I felt its cold temperature compared to the humid air, but remembered it was a simulation and moved on to the next item.

A tremendous pile of leaves stood before me. From their strange colours and the way they glittered, I knew they weren't regular leaves. I had a sudden urge to pick one up and did so.

The leaf disintegrated into glitter powder once I touched it and stained my fingertip yellow. I sighed and moved on to the next one. It was a set of five, damp wood logs placed perfectly on top of each other. The next was a thatched basket full of soft, white feathers. The feathers glowed brightly, emitting a positive aura.

The last item was a fiery red leather book. When I opened it, there was nothing inside and I sighed, having hoped for something like a message, anything to tell me what to do next. I decided to continue in the direction I had been heading before I stumbled upon the selection of items.

As soon as I started running again, a force sent me flying back to the field and I landed with a thump on my back.

"Ah..." I groaned.

When I got up, I noticed the fog closing in.

It was already past the snowman and was coming towards me at a creepily fast pace. Vibrations were sent through my arm; when I checked the timer, it showed my time was up. The snowman was nowhere to be seen, the fog had consumed it as if it was never there. I felt a strong sense of fear as it consumed the logs. It was getting too close to me for comfort.

I tried to escape through the bushes, but the force threw me back again. Once the fog got too close, I teleported back to the trees, only to still end up inside the fog. It was my first time successfully teleporting without her help, except I couldn't help but feel frustrated that everywhere I turned there was fog. It was so thick I couldn't even see myself. It was obvious that my memory would have to take me from here. Grammie said that the round would end when I'd teleported to each object I saw.

When I'd teleported the first time, it wasn't something I had been sure about. I'd been high on adrenaline and magic but now I wasn't sure if I could do it again.

I started with the trees, remembering their chips and the markings I had put on them, then watched as the fog cleared from them. Was the aim to remove the fog?

I teleported to the snowman, then to the wood logs, then to the glittering pile of leaves. Each time I teleported, it became easier. Now, when I called to my magic, it came to me instantly. When I'd reached the book, I realised why this level was so easy; it was because the items stood out and were easy to find. I teleported to the basket full of feathers as it was the last item, and then stood there panting as the simulation faded away.

I thought I would see Grammie when the simulation faded; instead, all I saw was darkness.

I stood up and scanned around to see if there was anything there. After a short while, the orange dots appeared, and I mentally prepared myself for the task at hand.

They had formed a huge pulsing sphere in front of me and after a few seconds, it exploded, scattering them all over the vast space.

After a short while, I was immersed in the simulation of a cave.

The cave was covered in algae and there was water dripping from the ceiling. It was a sign that wherever I was, the air was humid. Once I'd reset the timer on my wrist, I sauntered into the cave and my sight adjusted to the darkness. The cave had a straight path, so it was easy to navigate. With my triphant vision, I could make out glowing plants scattered in the path. Their unique glow and rare colours lured me in; I didn't want to take my eyes off of them.

Soon I was following the path of the flowers instead.

They led me to a section that was flowing with crystal clear, luminescent water. I waded through its freezing water, lifted my head, and peeked over the crashing water to see yet another obstacle course.

This time it was a jungle with vines hanging from trees that towered hundreds of feet above the cave, covering most of the arctic blue sky. The jungle was humid and there was the constant screech of some kind of bird.

I squinted to see what was beyond the fog of the trees, but when I couldn't, I knew the only way to find out was to head down there. I had had enough of the water crashing down on my head, so I retreated into the humidity of the cave. I hadn't seen anything inside of it, so I resorted to jumping off the obsidian, slippery ledge into the unknown fog.

I landed harshly in the river and pulled the water off me like I'd been taught. The water gathered into a huge bubble; once I released my control over it, the bubble fell away, and the water became one with the river once again.

The fog was gathering once again until there was one obvious path of moist dirt. The floating trees created shadows of leaves on the ground and the sun shone through the little gaps there. Beads of sweat began to form on my forehead thanks to the sweltering heat. As I got deeper into the jungle, I could make out more birds chirping and monkeys screeching. Though I heard the roar of a jaguar nearby, there was no living creature in sight, not even insects. The thought of them being invisible sent chills down my spine, but I kept going down the path, trusting Grammie to keep me safe. I ended up convincing myself that the simulation had put the sounds there for the effect of the jungle.

The land stretched on for miles and blurred into the distance. On my left, I spotted a glistening object and went over to check it out.

It was a spacesuit helmet in the middle of the tropics. I was glad it was strange as I needed all the help I could get with remembering the objects to teleport to; there was no telling how many more I would have to memorise. I checked the time; it read "*15 29*". I still had time but not enough at the pace I was going. Thankfully, unlike the trees back in level 1, I wouldn't have to memorise the exact location they were in, just the object itself. After the helmet, it was a golden nugget, along with a sack of rice, and then I found a metal door standing by itself.

I opened it but there was nothing on the other side. I sighed and continued. The next few objects blurred together, and soon I saw a marketplace in the distance. It resembled the one in my dream, but it was built with different materials, most likely from the resources available in the forest. The closer I got, the more I could make out the abundance of items stocked on the tables. When I got up close to the stalls, I trailed my hands along the rotting wood holding the woven baskets filled with fruits and vegetables. There were three baskets in total, filled with various foodstuffs that could have only been taken from the jungle itself.

When I walked back to the path, the ground shook, forcefully throwing me back to the side of a stall. The thud disturbed the dirt all around me, creating gusts of dirt clouds. In a matter of seconds, the trees that had been floating had dropped to the ground leaving little space for me to escape. It was clear this was where the test would start. In order to get past this barricade, it was clear I needed to teleport to somewhere beyond the trees;

and my thoughts instantly flashed to the objects I'd seen on the plains.

I closed my eyes and called on the familiar cool rush of magic to teleport to the first item, the helmet. When I reached the helmet, the same trees as before crashed around me; after that, each time I teleported to the next item, they surrounded me. I was tiring fast, but I continued to teleport to the various items until I was back to the door that I'd opened before. But there was something different about the door this time. The door glowed white and, when I turned the knob, I was taken to the next level.

At first, all I could see were swirls of thick silvery mist. I knew to reset my clock before doing anything and watched as the time started to tick down from "30 *00*".

In the distance, I heard soft theme music and, as I walked further into the setting, I saw the source, a carousel.

My muscles ached from the last level, but I ignored them and continued. I passed a bold sign that read, "**Welcome to FreeFair**". Beside it, there was a vivid drawing of a clown with a big red ball stuck on its nose. As I got closer to the carousel, I noticed two streetlights illuminating the horses in their different spots, equally spaced from each other.

As I walked up to the raised platform and touched the cool surface of the porcelain horse, the hazy, silver mist cleared and other scenes were revealed. I saw a stall with water guns positioned towards targets and an abundant source of teddy bears. But before I headed over there, I absorbed the details of the intricate patterning of the horses and their different colours. I memorised one horse in particular; its lilac-blue colour and patterned waves and clouds stood out the most.

I hurried onto the next station, where I memorised the different-sized swirls in the pattern on the gold-painted wooden surface. But one thing that caught my attention about this stall was the biggest fluffy stuffed animal. It was a bunny with a smile fixated on its face. Its outer fur was pink and its inner fur was white. I would remember its big black eyes that seemed to stare into the depths of my soul.

I skipped over to the next stall selling food. My eyes skimmed over a golden sign with big, black lettering that read **"Snacks and Beverages"**. My mouth watered at the sight of the glazed popcorn labelled as "caramel corn". I almost forgot it was a simulation. The cotton candy came in three colours, yellow, pink and blue. There were also two flavours of slushies and different cups to drink them in. The labels for the slushy machine read **"Blue Raspberry"** and **"Cherry Bomb"**.

The popcorn stood caramelized in its clear tub. The lighting inside further highlighted how crunchy it looked. My mouth watered from seeing it and I almost forgot it was a simulation.

In the distance, I spotted a red, green and white circus tent. I moved on past it, as I thought that just the exterior would be enough of a visual memory for me to teleport to it. However, then I saw another two circus tents that had the exact same designs. I went back to the first one I had skipped and ventured inside. When I entered, there was the loud noise of a crowd chattering. Inside there were many rows of vacant seats laid out as if a show was about to happen. It was just the absence of people that made it more abnormal.

The stage was round and illuminated by yellow stage lights. I climbed the steps and skidded around on the smooth, polished wooden surface. I walked to the middle of it and closed my eyes, feeling the warmth of the stage lights streaming through my eyelids. I imagined myself as a performer who had just finished a show and was receiving passionate cheers from the imaginary crowd.

The moment didn't last for long, as I knew the time for this level would run out soon. I checked the timer and it read "*16 52*". I hurried on to the next tent, which turned out to be a drastic change from the other.

In this tent, there was a tightrope set up high above the ground, almost as if there was a show happening. Unlike the other tent, this one was eerily silent and lacked the chatter of a typical audience.

All was dark except for the stage and I heard the occasional sound of awe from the audience. That was all I needed to realise what was going on. In real life, the crowd would be watching circus performers walk the tightrope. I hurried out, knowing I would remember the tent, which was dark except for the pink stage lights that shone onto the stage.

The next tent wasn't far away. Once I pulled the curtain entrance aside, I saw that there was nothing inside; it was just a stagnant, empty space gathering dust. It was rather disappointing, but it also meant there was less to memorize. I hurried to the next station that read '**Magic Mirrors**'. The title gave me a predetermined idea of what I would see inside the small, purple building. My shoes clicked against the wooden floor as I walked towards the metal door.

I grabbed the silver doorknob and twisted it. It was cold and smooth. The door opened to reveal the many mirrors inside. Once I stepped in, it immediately slammed shut. I was bombarded with various reflections of myself in the many mirrors. I looked deep into my hazel eyes and realised that my veins were glowing pink. I blamed it on the fact that I had been using my power so much; in fact, teleporting had now become almost second nature to me.

It was when I blinked out of the trance I was in that I realised my grave mistake. I had taken a step forward and that was all I had needed to get trapped in the world of mirrors. I felt a few seconds of sheer panic before I realised I could just teleport out. I envisioned the food stall; when I appeared in front of it, there was fog all around me. I gasped and looked at the timer, which read "7 59". There was still time so I didn't know why I was being surrounded. Did the time reduce each time I teleported or was there something else I didn't know? The fog had engulfed the entire landscape and cut my exploration short. I teleported to the things I had ventured to, the blue porcelain horse in the carousel, the circus tents, the teddy bear stall and lastly the mirror building. When I arrived in the world of mirrors, the place didn't fade away and no doors materialised to take me to the next level. I glanced at the timer; it read '7 25'. I hadn't run out of time so there was only one conclusion. I hadn't explored everything. I gasped as I remembered the one ride in the distance. It was the same rollercoaster I had meant to visit right after the world of mirrors but, of course, that hadn't happened.

My time continued to count down and I could only make things up in my head. It took me three attempts, after all of which I ended up in the fog to realise that I was not passing this level. Instead, I sat down in the fog for a few more seconds until it cleared and I was back in the training chambers with Grammie standing in the distance clapping. "Well done. You managed to get to level four on your first try. I couldn't say the same for your mother." She chuckled.

My smile went away as quickly as it appeared when I asked, "What about Red?"

She paused and then admitted, "She reached level 6." I sighed. "I…"

"Don't compare yourself to Red. Her ability makes her teleporting powers stronger than any other of the chosen. You should be proud you got that far with no experience of teleporting yourself."

"Yes, Grammie." She crouched down and pressed the back of her hand lightly to my forehead. "Do you feel okay? Strong enough to practise portal jumping?" For once, she wasn't her calm self; I sensed she was feeling fear.

"I feel warmed up," I said. It wasn't a yes or no answer, but it was true. I was one with my magic and it felt exhilarating. It was coming as soon as I searched for it. I stood up slowly and stretched. From my past experience, portal jumping had the same essential nature s teleporting, but it took a lot more strength. But Grammie was right about the game, it had helped strengthen my memory and the way I used it to coordinate with my magic. I listened to her as she repeated the instructions for portal jumping. I grounded myself and channelled my magic into the image I had summoned into my head. I took a deep breath, as usual, to keep my focus and clear my head.

These were all the things I had attempted to master in the past, but when your magic felt as smooth as silk, everything just felt better and stronger. Before, my photographic memory was just a thing in the back of my head that I never used, but now I understand it. After years of being left in the dark, I was finally starting to understand who I was and what I was capable of doing. There were a couple of things I had grown accustomed to in Clorista, especially the warm oak doors to my chambers. I envisioned myself entering using the light touch of my palm. I envisioned the cool surface of the marble tiles that silenced my steps. In my mind, I was slowly creating my chambers. I was looking up at the diamond ceiling, but it was dark so I used the tourmaline wall lights beside the door that activated the peach opal lights hanging from the jasmine-white ceiling. I walked further into the room and the arched entryway to the bathroom appeared. I walked past Nora and the white walls, into the gold bathroom. The first thing I saw was the round bath with jets that I would occasionally use. In my mind, there were puddles on the floor, so I switched the setting of the floor to evaporate, one of the things Nora had taught me recently.

It amazed me every time that the water would dry up almost instantly. Usually, I would have to use my magic to protect myself from the heat, but I couldn't feel anything in my mind, only the essence of it. So, I stood there looking at the disappearing water until my gaze flickered to the glistening golden sink and the shiny, tinted mirror I would stare into for a few seconds every day.

The intricately-decorated porcelain strip dragged along all the white ceramic walls. There was a translucent barrier between the sleek shower head that seemed to have countless settings. Other than the tubes of soap that would fill themselves up every so often, that was it for the bathroom, so I headed out. I skimmed the dressing table to my left that had an oval mirror, along with a tiny chair to sit in front of it. Then it was the windows that were always squeaky clean and clear as ever to enhance the experience of virtual reality. It was actually a single window that stretched around the front of the room, framed with gold patterns. I visualised the glowing yellow ball that would shine into my bedroom every day. It only ever went away when I shut the lights off and the windows became tinted.

I moved away from the window and towards the doors that would automatically open for me. I had become quite accustomed to my wardrobe and often rearranged it when I felt it got too boring. The last time I rearranged it, everything had been colour-coded, down to the hair clips. I slid the shoe shelves aside to reveal the large mirror, just as I had the first time I explored it. I saw my past self – as bony as ever, with my cheekbones protruding, and significantly less strength.

I shivered, thinking about it. I hurried out of the wardrobe and was drawn back to my state of deep focus, more connected to the location of my chambers than ever. I imagined the connection as a rope and grabbed hold of it. Once it held strong, I stepped into the portal I had been creating and opened my eyes. I let out a gasp at the thought that I had finally made it to my chambers.

I had successfully portal jumped and I couldn't help but feel satiated.

Grammie appeared in front of me and smiled. "How was that for you?"

I sighed with relief and replied, "It was good." It was true, it had been nothing like the first time I had tried. "I feel a bit worn out but... I don't feel like collapsing and crying so that's an improvement."

I laughed with her and she teleported away knowing she would see me again when it was time for our history lesson.

CHAPTER 22

GREEN

Instead of the waiting realm, she took us to a cave. I didn't say anything. I couldn't find the will to talk. "You'll be safe here," she said.

I mustered enough energy to look up at her bony self. There were a number of things I could have said; instead, I stayed silent. She didn't say much but kept addressing me as Green no matter how many times I told her that my name was Kyung-Dae.

"I shall have to leave now, Green."

I had been ignoring her until she said that. "What?" I replied.

"I am needed elsewhere and I have delivered you to the location they gave me, therefore my job here is done."

"Just like that?" My heart had caught in my throat.

"Your loneliness will only be temporary. Your ride will be

here soon. She is known as Pink. She is also one of the chosen, like you."

"But what do I do? How long is 'soon'?"

"In the meantime, find your gemstone. You'll barely notice the time pass."

I tried to think of something to make her stay, but my mind was blank. I watched as a golden portal opened in front of her and she left.

I felt the pinprick feeling cease; the place seemed to grow colder and goosebumps coated my skin. I got up from leaning on the wall and dusted myself off.

Find your gemstone.

I never learned her name. All I knew was that she had been working at my school as a nurse, just waiting for this moment. So she would always be known as 'the lady who ruined my life'.

I turned away and searched for the exit. It was easy enough. There was only one source of light and it was coming from straight ahead. I recognised the bridge beyond the tunnel entry and my heart caught in my throat. I was still in Jinhae. I tried to leave of course, but something prevented me from stepping foot outside of the entrance. Instead, I was thrown back onto the rocky ground, bruising another part of my body with every attempt.

I was about to try again, this time running into the force to see if I could break past it when I heard voices. They seemed to swarm me with their whispers.

"Green... Green..." They chanted.

I was being summoned.

I followed the whispers, getting glimpses of a glowing stone floating somewhere.

It was a bright, mesmerising green.

It might have led me to my death, but it wasn't like there was anyone alive who cared about me. I could die and no one would know.

The cave went deeper than I had expected it to. There were winding tunnels that never seemed to end. I could have been walking for days for all I knew. All that mattered was finding the gemstone that was rightfully mine. I didn't know when my strong desire to find the gemstone had materialised. All I knew was there and I needed it.

I finally spotted a soft glow in the distance. The pull was stronger than ever. Fog spilled down the narrow path. Once I'd got close to it, I took it from its floating spot. Memories flashed before my eyes; some I'd forgotten about and others I could never forget, no matter how hard I tried. At the end of the memories was a vivid image of me with glowing green eyes.

The gemstone was warm and its pulse was soothing. Holding it made me feel complete as if I had been missing something my entire life. I returned to the same spot where the lady had left me and sat down on the rocky ground. I leaned on the cool wall and studied the fine details of the gemstone. It had intricate lines engraved on its surface. They resembled symbols, but I couldn't be sure.

Beyond that was a green light that danced around in the gemstone.

It was a bright, enchanting green.

It was mesmerising but, the more I waited here, the more I felt myself becoming disconnected from reality. It was as if I was living in a fever dream, except the rocks on the floor felt too sharp, the air was too moist and the wall felt colder than ever. I felt trapped and helpless. I was stuck in a dank cave with no way out. I had no one and nothing to trust except the words of the lady. It was anyone's worst nightmare.

CHAPTER 23

PINK

I was at the towering doors once again. They swung open as usual and I saw books zooming from one end of the library to another.

I spotted Grammie on a levitating platform high up in the air. "You need books to read and knowledge to absorb when I'm not available," she started, "Resources that are more detailed and thorough. That way, you'll understand more and come to me with any questions you may have."

"OK," I said as I sat at the table.

"Finally," she muttered.

I saw a glimmering gold book hover towards her until she had it clasped in her hands. She climbed down from the platform, strolled over and handed it to me.

It was heavy and felt warm. I smiled, excited to read my first book from the library. I attempted to open it and furrowed my eyebrows when I realised it wouldn't let me.

"I instructed it not to open until you got back to your chambers."

"Oh," I muttered, "Of course it follows instructions."

I sighed and put it down beside me.

She took a seat opposite to me. "As you are retrieving Green, there are things you must be wary about, including his powers." Her voice was firm and she had on a serious expression.

I nodded in response and she continued, "The green gemstone deals with antimagic." My eyes widened, I had never heard that term before but it sounded like a threat. She nodded. "Yes, it is a threat, to you and every single magical being that exists. He has the ability to undo any spell, combat any magic you may try using, and even sever your connection with your magic." I gasped, my fear probably showing on my face, as she quickly reassured me, "He will not be able to do that unless he is trained to do so, until then it would remain an unknown power."

I let out a breath I hadn't known I was holding and she went on to say, "However, despite magic being useless against him, there are some powerful concoctions made with non-magical ingredients from various places. His magic will be wild and unrefined, Adira. It is imperative you stay alert at all times. No hesitation, understood?"

"Yes, Grammie."

"Now come along." She strode off and I followed. I couldn't help but feel excited about the mystery of the journey. She could have teleported us to where she was going. Instead, she led me through bright hallways that got progressively darker as we ventured into sections I'd never seen. Somewhere along the way, torches appeared and there was a holder from which she grabbed one for herself – so I did the same. The fire illuminated etchings of stick men on the bronze stone wall. From what I saw, it looked like a story being told. I had got so lost in analysing it, that I didn't realise I'd stopped. "Adira," Grammie called. In the middle of hurrying to catch up with her, I felt as if I had run through a sheet of cold water and tripped on a decent-sized stone. I looked around and realised I was in some sort of dank cave with water that glowed a bright, arctic blue. The smell had changed as well, from the faint sweet scent of Clorista to petrichor.

"Welcome to the enchantment chambers," Grammie announced, "This is where potions are brewed and concoctions are made."

"Why is it a cave?"

"For safety precautions… Some potions may cause explosions. The cave is built to withstand that."

"Oh… Where's the equipment?"

She snapped her fingers and it materialised in front of me. There were two cauldrons, an opulent white desk, and a shelf filled with different commodities. I assumed they were ingredients for making spells.

"Wow…" I murmured. I was excited to use a cauldron for the first time. I had always wondered what it would be like.

"Today you will learn to make sleeping powder. It's one of

the simpler things to make, so you should grasp the concept given that you're a fast learner."

"I'll try," I said.

I was heading towards the cauldron when she said, "You will not be using cauldrons today. Instead, you will be using a mortar. She snapped her fingers once again and the cauldrons disappeared. The disappointment probably showed on my face.

"Don't worry – there will be times you'll get to use a cauldron… just not this time," she assured me.

"OK," I muttered in resignation.

"Now." She clapped her hand twice and glowing green orbs appeared twinkling in the ceiling. They cast a lime glow onto the place. "These are crystalline orbs, enchanted to reveal the pH of a solution. When you get to the more sophisticated levels of enchantment, they will assist you."

"How exactly do they assist me?" I asked.

"Look at the shelves. What do you see?"

I glanced at the shelves to see that though the items were different colours, they ranged from the colours red to purple. "All of the tubes with liquid have changed to colours ranging from red to purple."

She nodded. "Exactly that. Red represents those with acid while blue represents those with alkaline. Once your mixture is neutral, it will stop glowing."

She pointed to a different section. "When it comes to the solids, it is important that you pay attention to the amount you are instructed to use and exactly how." She snapped her fingers

BECOMING PINK

and the book she had given me appeared on the table. "This book is a grimoire, you'll be using it today."

"OK." I looked through it; the spells were structured like recipes. It was almost as if I was baking something.

I frowned and asked, "Which page is it on?" I looked around and she had disappeared – but I trusted she hadn't gone far.

The pages flicked to a specific one and I muttered, "Thanks."

I looked down at the recipe to read the list of ingredients.

ITEMS:

- Lavender
- Waun
- Tyraux tears
- Min dust
- Venmar
- Tam

Once I'd successfully found all the ingredients and laid them out in front of me, I started on the first step. It involved taking two tablespoons of Waun, a sticky, purple liquid with the consistency of honey. After reading through the instructions, I realised that I wouldn't be needing the mortar until I added the Tyraux tears.

For now, I used a bowl and mixed a pinch of min dust into the waun, turning the mixture from violet to a pale shade of mauve. The mi dust was an orange and white grainy substance.

It didn't seem to do anything but I kept stirring. The Min dust thickened it and caused it to bubble a little. I kept stirring with the silver spoon as it said until the mixture eventually began to harden.

When I took off the clear lid from the jar containing the tam, a rancid smell wafted into my nostrils, almost making me puke. It was a goo-like pale green substance. I watched as it took forever to drop from the spoon, not bothering to question what purpose it served. After it had finally dropped in, I enjoyed the amusement of watching the mixture change colour as I stirred it, from mauve to baby blue.

The final step was to add the Tyraux tears, which had a faint sweet scent. I put three drops in, just as it had said, and watched as the mixture fizzed.

I set an internal timer for two minutes while I worked on grinding the copper leaves from the Venmar plant in the mortar. Just as the recipe said they would, the leaves disintegrated after I applied a certain amount of force to them. After a short while, the five leaves I used had been reduced to an amber powder. Just as I was dusting off my hands, I felt a vibration in my wrist. The timer had finished.

I used the pestle to tap on the hardened mixture and watched in satisfaction as it all collapsed into emerald-green powder underneath the layer of film. I peeled off the green layer and mixed in the amber powder. As the amber dust scattered amongst the mini particles of the powder I grinned to myself knowing I had successfully made my first sleeping potion – or so I thought.

Grammie appeared almost as soon as I'd finished mixing and I turned to her with a beaming smile. "I did it!"

"Let's see." She grabbed some and blew it on me before I could react. I panicked and blacked out before I could register what she'd just done.

My eyelids fluttered open and I stared at the cave ceiling. Grammie stood looming over me. "You were only out for thirty seconds. Not enough Tam or Waun. Try again." She smirked and remarked, "Thought it would be that easy?"

"I..." I knew I had to do it again. I groaned and she snapped her fingers, making the powder disappear.

"That was disappointing," I muttered and felt her presence leave once again.

I repeated the steps, this time faster, since I knew what I was doing, careful with the amounts I was adding; this time I stood there for the painstakingly long time it took for the Tam to drop off the spoon. I ground the leaves once again and mixed that into the powder. My hands shook as I handed her the bowl of powder this time. All the confidence I had had was gone, replaced with the fear that it wouldn't work.

"What if it lasts too long?" I asked.

"There are antidotes..." I let out the sigh I'd been holding. "But the side effects of using too much of something will remain."

I racked my head, trying to remember how much Tam I had added this time. I remembered the globs I had thrown in because it was taking too long. I gasped and shouted, "Wait." But it was too late, she'd already blown it into my face.

I woke up on my bed and got up fast, instantly regretting it. My head was throbbing and my vision was dancing.

"Movement detected. Calling Crystiana." I heard Nora announce.

After a few seconds, there were knocks at the door and I groaned in response, too weak to say anything else. She strolled in, walked up beside me and ordered, "Drink this."

I recognised the bronze liquid swirling in the silver cup.

Crystal water.

I took the cup from her and gulped the familiar silky liquid that felt so cool down my throat. I felt the headache ebb away. "Thank you," I said.

"No problem. You were out for about two hours. I'd say it's successful enough. The powder was too acidic, which is why you woke up with a headache."

"I realised I added too much Tam…"

"But it was too late," she said, interrupting me.

"Yeah…"

"We'll use it though, given that it works. Crystal water will solve the side effects he'll experience but you must practise this spell for the next time you need it. It comes in very handy when it comes to wanting to defeat your enemies. Bear in mind this does not work for certain magical creatures. That is why you need to work on your fighting skills."

"I understand."

"Hopefully you won't encounter any magical creature other than Green."

"Hopefully."

She lifted my chin with a gentle gesture and whispered, "Rest up. We have a few last things to do before you retrieve Green." I nodded. A few moments after she disappeared, I announced, "Nora, turn off the lights, please."

They shut off and I observed the aurora lights dancing on my ceiling. The anxiety of going to Earth on my own was creeping up on me.

What if I messed up?

CHAPTER 24

RED

*B*ellbon's atmosphere was light and warm.

Its court was surrounded by a river of iridescent water and opal tiles that were enchanted to absorb water stretched across the land. There were ice sculptures of influencers in the court stationed at various points where I had arrived. There were flags raised everywhere, all depicting the colours of the royal family.

There were scarce people around but that was because they were having a ceremony. The royal family was hosting a wedding. I didn't know who it was for but I knew it would impact the way that Lord Aenesty responded to me. I took one last look at the clear sky and glimmering water before I portalled to Tolken, an earth court. I made a mental note to go back to Bellbon. I was hoping that when I returned, the ceremony would be over.

The rocky soil crunched under my boots as I made my way to the capital. Fae flies buzzed around my ears. I swatted them away but that didn't stop them being any less of a nuisance.

Their only captivating feature were their lights. Each fly gave off its own patch of vibrant colour in the air.

It was sunset and swirls of purple and pink meshed together, filling the coral-coloured sky. It was entrancing.

Unlike the previous courts I'd visited, Tolken didn't have any fancy gates, but a solid wall that wrapped around their court. I reached the part of the wall where earth fae were stationed. They too recognised me and with the gesture of their hand, a section of the wall crumbled away, revealing the secluded village. I strolled in and briefly observed the dance the crowd was captured by. It was done by toned males wearing extravagant headwear decorated with all sorts of plants. It shook violently whenever they made a drastic move. They danced with the earth they pulled from the ground in swift movements.

They shaped it into something to tell their story. Their wrists and ankles glistened in the light as they were painted with gold. I smiled at the young faeries who were trying to replicate the same movements before portalling straight to Lord Bunter. He didn't have a castle, instead, he had a giant hut filled with earth fae hurrying around.

"Are you here to see Lord Bunter?" A deep voice from behind me asked.

I whipped my head around to see a female faerie with a scarf wrapped around her head. Just like most faeries, she towered over me by a few inches and looked down to me with her fuschia pink irises. Her cheekbones jutted out; it was a common feature for the earth faeries. Her chestnut brown skin was patterned with various intricate designs that depicted parts of Tolken. There were large, opal sea shells covering her breasts and a purple bush skirt that clung to her hips and stretched down to her ankles.

"Yes," I replied.

She nodded and headed to a dimly lit passage on the right. Her bush skirt swayed along, making a faint swishing noise every time she took a step. I followed right behind her, making sure to take in the detailed paintings placed every few metres on the birch walls alongside us. T

here were designs etched into the floor, most likely earth fae symbols. They were spelled for certain purposes, like secret passages. But could only be used a certain amount of times before they disappeared.

The earth faerie in front of me used one of them to open a door on the floor. It revealed a winding staircase that went a far distance down. We started walking down the steps, but once the door latch closed, she immediately waved her hands to create a floating platform from the rocks in the walls. It reminded me of the entry to Saphella's library.

She stepped onto it in a fluid motion and I followed.

It dropped steadily to the ground. On the way down, the staircase stopped abruptly and I understood why she created the platform. It was a good safety precaution for the most part. Once we reached the bottom, we hopped off and she led me to an open taupe cave-like space.

Light streamed down from the tiny holes above onto the centre where golden statues stood. They each represented a previous Tolken lord. They would all be worth a significant amount in the human world, but here they were just manipulated shiny rocks.

As we moved forward the entry to the open section was covered with by the wall as if it was never there and after a few more winding paths, we got to a section where a throaty laugh bounced off of the walls. When we took a turn, the source of the noise was a plump, male faerie. He had the same chestnut complexion as her.

"Get out!" He shouted at a servant and laughed some more, his round belly shaking with each chuckle. He was getting his toes massaged by a male servant and his hands manicured by females.

The faerie who led me here cleared her throat and he looked up. "Fedelia, who is it you bring to me?" He asked.

"I believe it is one of the chosen."

"Hm." He gestured to his servants to leave and said, "Thank you, Fedelia. You may leave."

She sauntered away and I waited until I could no longer feel their auras to say, "War is coming. One that will dictate the fate of the universe. It will take place in the motherland. You must gather your troops and warn your people. There's no knowing when the sides of chaos will attack."

He was dead silent and then laughed. "I don't know what to say."

"Say you will gather your troops and ensure the safety of your people. This was prophesied to happen by Present. You must do what you can to save as many lives as possible. This is not something you can hide from, Lord Bunter and as one of the Lord's of the faerie realm, you are obligated to choose peace."

"And if I don't?"

Hot bubbles rose in my stomach. The heat travelled fast around my body and red sparks appeared, dancing in my palm. "You dare question me?"

He gulped. "I will gather my troops."

I glared at him with enough intensity for it to be scarred into his memory and portalled back to Bellbon, and then Ellyon, then finally Augustine, where I was met with a chilly wind that bit at my bare skin. I asked my gemstone for warmth and felt it wrap my body with its warm, red sparks.

My reflection stood staring at me from the ice and beyond it, I saw the ethereal hues of the sky. The stars sung in the velvet carpet of magenta, violet and indigo blue.

The ice had water fae symbols etched into it and glowed blue around my feet, recognising my magic. A few metres in front of me, a pair of male faeries hurried inside the palace. I walked up to the towering doors and they opened slowly, revealing the faerie lord sitting on a very rigid-looking throne. It was made up of shards of ice and lined with some type of white fur. His platinum blond hair had two braids at the front, whilst the rest reached down to his elbows; the ends were cut in an immaculate, straight line.

"Ah... I've heard news of your visit," he started, his raspy voice amplified by the room.

"Come to tell me about the prophecy?"

"Yes, Lord Lucius, I have. But it seems there is no need to use my time here as you already know. I trust you will gather your troops for the side of peace." I was about to portal out when he said.

"Actually... I was thinking we could discuss the best course of action over dinner. It's already been made."

"I should really get going," I said.

"Oh, but if we're about to go into war, this might be the last homemade meal in a while and I bet it's been a long trip, so do stay if only for a little bit."

"I-," I paused. He had caught my attention by mentioning a homemade meal. I hadn't eaten one of those in a while and the stress of war was getting to me.

"I'll only be able to stay a little while."

He made a gesture with his hands. "Fine by me." He stood and the sheer train from his light blue gown dragged along behind him.

Two faeries escorted me. They towered over me by a few

feet. Their height is what reminded me that Lord Lucius' army was among the most powerful and strategic out of all the courts. The detailed design of the dining room was admirable and managed to make every inch of the vast space seem majestic. Unlike the dull glow of the throne room, the bright chandelier cast a gold hue on everything. There was a glass table that stretched across the centre of the room. Despite it being able to hold a decent number of people, there were only a few plates and cutlery put down. It was just the right amount for Lord Lucius, the two faeries and me. I sat at the far end of the table, opposite to Lucius, while the two faeries split up and sat beside one of us.

The food was placed in front of us by other faeries wearing furry aprons as well as their cobalt blue attire. He made a gesture to say thank you and picked up a piece of glazed steak with a silver knife. I did the same and groaned as the flavours exploded in my mouth.

"It's good, isn't it?"

"Mhm…" I closed my eyes to appreciate the flavour even more. "I remember the… last… time…" My eyelids grew heavy. Too heavy.

I drew magic from my gemstone but it was too late. They stayed shut and I drifted until an all-encompassing darkness embraced me.

I WOKE UP IN A CELL, barred with mercury. I breathed heavily and felt hot rage. It was so hot it burned and all I saw was red.

The two faeries at the sides of the cell disappeared and the bars of the cell as well. I portalled back to the throne room where I felt Lord Lucius' aura had disappeared from a long time ago. I rushed outside. It was daylight.

My blood boiled with fury.

"BETRAYER!" I screamed at the top of my lungs. I made the mistake of falling for the tricks of a cunning faerie lord. He had managed to outsmart one of the only magical beings capable of destroying him.

But he had now revealed where his loyalties lied. I recalled the sly grin he wore when he spoke and the lack of emotion in his cold, calculating gaze. I didn't think much of his pale blue eyes, but they seemed too indifferent to be genuine.

I portalled back to Autumn. The streets were strangely silent and hardly any faeries were out. I was pleased to see Lord Theo had taken action and headed straight to Madella's underground castle where I found Saphella absorbing purple magic.

Madella's purple magic.

"Saphella, what have you done?" My heart caught in my throat as I looked at the grey patch of dust sitting in front of her and then at her. "Tell me. Now," I said through gritted teeth.

Though Saphella must have felt on top of the world with her new power, her face was crestfallen. She was a good actress, I'd give her that.

"Razel betrayed us," she said.

"Obviously!" I yelled, "I warned you both. What happened in my absence?"

"She confronted him- not long after you left- and then he

gave her this stupid speech that made her all sappy and she let her guard down..."

"Did you kill her?" I already had a ball of magic gathering in my palm.

"No... No, I didn't. It wasn't like that."

"Then what the hell happened?"

"She let her guard down and Razel escaped. Then... Then..." She hung her head and went silent.

"Then what?" I questioned. I couldn't deal with these emotions; too much was at stake.

She continued to look at the ground as she spoke, "She paid more attention to me than she ever had." She met my anger with an intense gaze and continued, "She gave me her power, Red and she meant it. She said it was her blessing and her eternal apology for what she'd put me through." Blue tears welled up in her eyes, threatening to spill. "He knows we're onto him. He muttered something about warning Lucius," she continued.

"Lucius slowed me down, that's for sure."

I still suspected something more, but I couldn't let her stay here, not with all of this power. I could no longer sense Madella's safety spells and that meant I wasn't the only one who could sense her.

"What now?" Her eyes were wide and frantic. Her green skin was no longer pale green but emerald, glimmering with magic. Saphella was already powerful as Madella's daughter and gaining her power had increased her potential by tenfold. It also made her a ticking time bomb just waiting to go off. I may not have known what she was capable of yet, but I knew one thing. Once she used it, she wouldn't be able to stop.

"You're coming with me," I said. It definitely wasn't something I had planned for, but that's what this life was all about, dealing with things you never expected to deal with.

"Okay."

"One last thing," I said.

She followed me as I went down the broad passage, to the confined room Madella had locked me in when I had first arrived. I cringed at how weak I was back then, and at how clueless I was. The door swung open with the flick of my wrist. "It's time."

"Red!" Sar exclaimed. Her eyes brightened up when she saw me and Clover gasped.

"We thought you weren't gonna come back for us," Nat admitted.

"Well, I did," I said.

Instantly crushing any doubtful thoughts they may have had, I shattered the jars they were in. The shards made a loud crashing noise as they were reduced to smithereens. Sar's wings fluttered but failed to keep her in the air and she fell to the ground. I made a bubble to catch her, using a trick from Madella's grimoire. I did the same for Nat and Clover.

"Thanks so much, Red. We're forever in your debt," Clover said, her eyes welling up with tears.

"All you have to do is help me out in this war."

"Okay," they chanted in unison.

I smiled and joined all of their bubbles into one. They

wrapped each other into an embrace. "That should keep you guys contained for now."

The portal I had made, pulsed in front of us and Sar asked, "Where are we going?"

"To Clorista," I said and stepped into the portal, Saphella following closely behind.

CHAPTER 25

PINK

I was drifting through a hazy fog, like I always did when I was in the subconscious realm when I heard a myriad of distant voices shouting. Soon the fog cleared up and I could see floating embers and a crowd that seemed to stretch on forever. They were cheering something. It took a couple of seconds for me to figure out I was back in the demon realm, and the cheering crowd was made up of demons.

Was this another message from Jake?

I headed closer to the stage where the attention was focused. I needed to see what this was all about. When I finally got to a level where I could see the stage clearly, I saw intricate drawings that seemed to have been drawn with ink. I hoped it was ink. It was were symbols that emitted an ominous aura. It sent violent shivers down my spine. I sensed magic but it was bitterly consuming.

Was this dark magic?

I recognised the bronze stone walls, but it was as if everything had been darkened to create the effect that the stage had a spotlight on it. There was no light streaming from above, but the stage itself was glowing. It caught me off guard when the crowd instantaneously went silent. I heard drums beat and their volume sent harsh vibrations throughout.

Dust fell and the ground cracked. The anticipation gnawed at me and my heart dropped when I heard her voice. It echoed and bounced off the surrounding walls. She was speaking another language entirely, but she sounded pleased. If this was Jake's mother, then anything she was happy about couldn't be good. The crowd split, and I split with them - afraid she would notice me somehow.

Her dark aura was so strong it was almost tangible. Even with the drums beating, my heartbeat seemed too loud. It seemed too noticeable and too human. Soon, she came into sight wearing a sheer black dress. It just preserved her modesty, and the split on her thighs stretched all the way to her hips. The black made her pale skin look like the colour had been drained out of it. The space grew increasingly cold as she approached. As she passed me she looked at me dead in the eyes and smirked. The smirk was cold and I felt my heart skip a beat.

She knew.

Her gaze flickered away from me, but her stare would forever be imprinted in my mind. I could hardly breathe from the stench of her magic and thanked the gods when she moved on. I let out the breath I'd been holding and my heart caught in my throat as I felt his presence.

My gaze shifted to the direction his mother had come from and there he was, his skin seeming to emit a blue hue. Unlike the previous time, when he had looked like he was on the verge of death, he'd been *given a makeover. His hair had grown much longer and his face had matured a lot from when I'd last seen him. It was chiselled almost, his baby fat gone. He had kohl outlining his upper eyelids that made the deep hue of his cerulean blue eyes more piercing than ever.*

His whole demeanour had changed as well, it was as if he'd finally accepted himself. His aura no longer felt conflicted.

It was my first time seeing him shirtless. He had grown significantly bulkier and I counted eight abs. I couldn't take my eyes off him. The way he was dressed, it was almost as if he was royalty. A chain of gold glistened on his collarbones and accentuated his pale complexion. As he passed me, I felt his power rolling off him in waves. Everyone seemed to shiver, but it embraced me. It engulfed me with a soothing warmth: the feeling that everything would be okay in the end.

Home.

"Jake..." His name left my lips by accident but his gaze flicked towards me. His eyes betrayed his emotion, despite his passive demeanour, but it was only for a second. He strolled up the steps to the platform, where his mother linked her arm with his. Together they climbed onto the platform and I moved to get a better angle.

He unlinked his arm from hers and stepped into the circle outlined with the strange black liquid. She closed it with a word and the drums immediately stopped beating. My ears rang from the sound. The silence was hard to get used to, but my attention was focused on Jake, as was everyone else's. Once he stepped into the circle, his mother started muttering words. It sounded like a spell. The liquid from the circle glowed royal blue and whispers floated through the room.

"Submit yourself," they said.

I could feel Jake's aura flicker. The veins in his face seemed to darken by the second. He was obviously struggling and I was trying to figure out what was causing his discomfort. His mother's chanting grew louder and so did the whispers. They hissed in my ears like snakes. Jake's eyes had been closed ever since the chanting had begun; when they opened it was almost as if it was by force. His eyes glowed blue and soon his veins did too. He looked visibly upset. Whatever his mother was doing was not something he wanted to do. I wanted to do something to ease the pain, so I sent a wave of reassurance down our bond, hoping he could feel it.

I didn't feel anything in response and I couldn't help but feel disappointed. Jake groaned in pain; soon it grew into a desperate cry for help. He fell to his knees and his hands curled into fists. His skin and hair were changing colour.

What was she doing to him?

Jake.

JAKE! *I called out to him, desperate for a response.*

I don't... want you... to see me like this, he replied.

It was weak but I could feel his pain through the bond. My heart ached and I wished I could wrap my arms around him. His pained expression triggered an intense hatred in me. I hated his mother. I hated the fact that she had taken him from me. I wanted to rip her apart and tear her to shreds. I tried drawing power from my gemstone, but I just grew weaker. It was in that moment that I realised that's what she had wanted me to do.

She laughed mockingly and I watched as Jake finished transforming.

The whispers stopped as soon as they started and in the silence, she announced, "On the anniversary of your birthing, you have been reborn into your true form."

She placed a black nestle crown onto his head and announced, "The prophecy has begun. My people, we are now closer than ever to restoring our power!"

Passionate cheers and shouts erupted from the massive crowd.

She lifted her arms up and shouted, "We will be in the shadows no longer!" She pointed to Jake and continued, "He is our hope. He will save us all."

I looked at Jake's new state. His honeycomb-coloured hair had turned jet black. His pale skin had turned cerulean blue with dark blue freckles scattered across it.

His eyes... His eyes were the same, thank the gods. His mother's malicious grin was terrifying enough to give me goosebumps.

Maybe this was more serious than I thought.

I WOKE up with a film of cold sweat coating my forehead. I wiped it off and headed to the bathroom to wash my face. My heart beat faster than usual and I hurried to get dressed. It was obvious I could no longer keep the messages Jake was sending me a secret. I had to tell Grammie what I'd seen.

∽

INSTEAD OF WALKING to the training chambers, I teleported. It was my new favourite way of getting around. "Grammie!" I called; when I turned around she was standing a few metres behind me.

"I'm here. What's the matter? You seem panicked." This time, she was wearing a white gown that flowed to the floor. Her caramel skin was decorated with gems that pulsed with magic, sparkling from the fluorescent lights.

"It's Jake."

Her eyebrows knitted together. "What about him?"

"He's been sending me these messages in the subconscious realm."

Her left eyebrow rose. "And you didn't tell me?"

"I'm telling you now." I ignored the purse of her lips and continued, "He sent me another one. This one was different. There was a huge crowd of demons in front of a stage with symbols drawn in black liquid. Jake's mother seemed happier than ever. Jake was dressed as if he was a prince. We all watched as they stepped onto the stage. Once he stepped into a circle drawn with the same black liquid, his mother started chanting this weird spell that sent whispers around. Whatever the spell was, it made Jake turn blue and his mother was saying things about a prophecy beginning."

"What you witnessed was dark magic, but you also witnessed the beginning of a war."

She teleported us to the library and brought a thick black book to the desk. The pages flipped by themselves and stopped at a page with cursive handwriting written in gold ink.

"About a millennia ago, Present prophesied that there would come a day when a hybrid is reborn into their natural state. On this day, the war between balance and chaos would begin," she started.

"Jake's a hybrid…"

"Who you witnessed being reborn." She turned the book around for me to see what it said. "I always knew this would happen, but I never expected it to be so soon."

I couldn't read the triphant language, so I skimmed the text and went straight to the drawings. They were sketches of Jake and me fighting. "These have appeared since I looked at it last."

"That's creepy. But, I don't understand. What does this mean?"

"No one can be sure of that as of now, but as time goes on, we will understand more. For now, it's obvious our timeline has moved up." She shut the book and then continued, "You need to hurry and master portal jumping. Green needs to be retrieved soon. A great evil is about to be unleashed, Adira. We're going to need everything we can get if we have any hopes of winning."

That's when it hit me. I was on the side of peace, but Jake…

We were fighting on opposite sides in a war that was bigger than both of us. All I could do now was hope that Jake didn't choose chaos in the end, but if he did…

I shivered at the thought of it. No matter what, I refused to fight him and I would do whatever it took to get him back.

But first, I needed to retrieve Green. The chosen triphant for anti-magic. The key to winning this upcoming war.

May the gods be with me.

THE CHOSEN TRIPHANTS
GREEN
THE RISE OF ANTIMAGIC

SURAIYA MATANDARA-CLARKE

THE CHOSEN TRIPHANTS: GREEN - THE RISE OF ANTIMAGIC

∼

Since the beginning of time, there has been balance. It's been up to the triphants to keep It and what they fought for millennia before. Last time, they had the advantage. But this time, a hybrid disturbs the order of nature and it will take more than the chosen to defeat the side of chaos. The odds are far greater than ever before and if they fail, the world as they know it will change forever.

Follow them as they discover the truth behind everything they've done.

Who can they trust? Will their powers be enough?

Chaos is threatening to take over and only they can stop it.

AFTERWORD

NOTE FROM THE AUTHOR:

Thank you so much for reading my book! I really hope you enjoyed it.

Feel free to ask me questions, tell me your favourite character or part, and maybe even things you think should happen in the next book. Please send it to suraiyamatandaraclarke@gmail.com

- Suraiya

ABOUT THE AUTHOR

Suraiya Matandara-Clarke discovered her love for writing at the age of 9 when she had finished reading her first fantasy series, *Harry Potter* by J.K. Rowling. It was at this age that she started writing her first book, *The Story of Margaret Mellow: The Origins of The Chosen*.

She lives in Kingston, Jamaica with her family and four cats. Living in places like England, New Zealand and Singapore has given her wide exposure to cultures that she brings out in characters and stories. She shows a great appreciation for diversity and tries her best to incorporate it into everything she writes. Making a world to escape to is her number one goal as she believes that's what makes a good book.

ALSO BY SURAIYA MATANDARA-CLARKE

The Story of Margaret Mellow: The Origins of The Chosen

The Chosen Triphants: Red

NOTES

Copyright © 2023 by Suraiya Matandara-Clarke

All rights reserved.

No part of this book may be reproduced in any form or by any electronic or mechanical means, including information storage and retrieval systems, without written permission from the author, except for the use of brief quotations in a book review.

Made in the USA
Columbia, SC
29 September 2023